Mark Mulle

PUBLISHED BY:

Mark Mulle

Copyright © 2019

To get a FREE book and be updated on Mark Mulle's books and latest releases, www.markmulle.com

TABLE OF CONTENTS

Book 1: Wrongly Accused

Day 1

Hey, name is Mark. I'm a humble farmer and a player who joined a brand new server just recently. I've been striving to survive on my own on these wild lands, but the struggle is real… getting by is hard sometimes, but I'm managing to do it.

Surviving is tough, especially when you are alone. During the day, I have to take care of my crops and look after them, build my house and also mine minerals to craft my tools. At night, I have to hole up inside my construction and watch out for the monsters that try to attack me.

Living in this world ain't easy... But it sure is pleasing. The beautiful sight brought along by the sun setting over the mountains... It's quite a view. If only I could get someone else to be with me, then things wouldn't be so lonely.

That's one of the reasons I started writing this diary. I've been feeling lonely lately, and now I can share my experiences and my daily life in this little book. So I guess I'll call this "Mark's Journal".

Day 2

Wow, I never knew living here alone was this hard! Y'know, I've been trying to build my own house, but I can't make it work. It's so hard, almost impossible. Mostly because, when I'm almost done with my house, the Creepers come around during the night and blow up next to me, taking out large chunks of the construction with them.

I hate Creepers! They always cause so much trouble for me. I mean, why do they explode? I guess I will never understand. Either way, I can't finish my house properly unless I find a way to keep the Creepers out.

I need to make a small wooden wall, or some sort of fence around the base so I can build my house in peace. I mustn't forget the torches, they're really important so the monsters don't spawn in this area.

I've always known the basics of this place, and I can get along pretty well. In fact, I have been playing since the Beta, but only returned recently. Lots of things have changed; new updates have rolled out... I feel kind of lost.

Anyway, I gotta get up on my feet again. I've joined this server and I won't back out easily. I need to practice my skills and train even more, because surviving here ain't easy. But I'll figure this out! I know I will... Somehow, I guess.

Day 3

Finally! I am really a genius! The fences did their job, and the Creepers didn't enter the area. I even worked during the night, because the monsters couldn't approach me at all. What a great idea!

First, I made a wooden fence and placed it around my house. Next, I made the fence two blocks tall to keep Skeletons away too. Now they can't shoot arrows at me, but I think I am vulnerable to Spiders... I guess they can climb the fence, but I haven't seen any lately.

Then, I built my house during the night as the Creepers and the Skeletons watched me from the fence, completely lost and disabled! Now that's a great victory for me. Mark, the great crafter, strikes again! My house is almost done now, thanks to the fences.

All walls and rooms are done. I need to finish the oak floor and then place the staircase roof to complete everything. When I am done with my beautiful house, I'll go get some Diamonds and Gold. I need better tools and weapons! Maybe an armor too, but that's too fancy for me right now. A simple set of tools should do just fine.

Anyway, I am free from the Creepers. That alone should be a good reason to be happy now, and to further improve my household. After that, my next plan is to search for other humans living around here.

I want to know if there are other people who, just like me, are living in this server and struggling with their daily chores.

Day 4

What the heck is wrong with these Creepers?! You know, when I thought everything was complete and I no longer had problems with the Creepers, those forsaken creatures came up from behind last night and exploded my fence! I was surrounded by the monsters and had to flee from the house with Creepers exploding next to me and Skeletons shooting arrows.

This morning, I came back to the house and there was not much left. My chest exploded with the house and the items inside were gone. They probably despawned during the night because they fell on the ground.

The house was in pieces... Most of the walls were down, there was a huge hole in the middle of the floor, and half of the fences were gone. This is just a tragedy... I was just out to get some items and those things creep up on me when I wasn't paying attention. I guess that's why they're called Creepers...

Anyhow, what should I do next? I am lost... I don't feel like rebuilding my house. I've tried several times and the Creepers always take me down. I am vulnerable and weak against those monsters, and I don't stand a chance against these creatures unless I've got some real tools and weapons with decent materials.

I guess I will follow my next plan, which is to find other humans living in this world. Maybe I can ask for help, they could assist me with my house. Living here by myself has become dangerous, and I am just wasting my own time rebuilding a house which will be constantly destroyed by a bunch of Creepers who come up out of nowhere.

Day 5

Today, I left my house (or what's left of it). I grabbed my belonging, a simple Iron sword and some torches, and wandered this world in hopes of finding other people living nearby. But I found nothing.

What's wrong? Aren't there any other players living here? Have they all left the server and I'm all alone here? No... Then the server would be completely inactive when I joined it for the first time.

Then maybe they're just living even farther. Or maybe they're living in another area... I don't know. I just want to find others that I can talk with.

Day 6

What a happy day! I finally found other humans, and also a place I can call home! As usual, I was wandering around, minding my own business, when I found a village in a jungle. How is that even possible?

I came into the jungle looking for an apple to eat when I saw the small houses. The village took advantage of the jungle's natural resources, with houses built over the huge trees and next to the small river amidst the jungle trees.

"Welcome, welcome!" A friendly player said.

29

"What is this place?" I asked him.

"This is a village of players who are living together in the jungle." He said.

"Great place and you must be the leader." I said.

"No, we don't have a leader! Here in this village, everyone has a say on things. We work together, we live together, and we survive together. That's how things work."

"Wow, that's really nice." I said. "Anyway, my name is Mark, and I've been looking for a place like this for a few days."

"Pleasure to meet you, Mark! My name is Joseph. You're welcome to stay here with us if you wish!"

"Really? That'd be great! Thank you for the offer, Joseph!" I said.

"You're welcome. Now come in! Let me introduce you to the other residents."

I met the other players and they were all nice to me. I felt home the moment I stepped onto this village. It's such a friendly and calm place, I am happier than ever now! I am sure Creepers will not be a problem anymore.

Day 7

Now that I am living in this village, I offered myself to help them in their daily chores.

"Very well Mark, so you want to work with us?" Joseph said.

"Yes I do! I'm thankful for being so well- received here, but I also want to lend a hand."

"That's nice, Mark. Well, in that case we always have an extra spot for working hands." Joseph said. "What are you good at?"

"Well, I am not a good builder, but I can deal with crops." I said.

"Crops? Nice! Crops sure come in handy. In fact, we don't have anyone here who works with crops. We get all of our food from fishing and also from an automated melon farm, but it would be nice to have different crops."

"Great. I'll get to work on it then!" I said.

"Very well, Mark. The house where you slept is your new home. You live next to the river's bed, and you can cultivate in that field next to the jungle's entrance. It's the only available place for a decent crop, and it's just a few feet away from the village."

"Alright. Thanks again for everything and I'll get on it!" I said.

My first day working with my crops was really good. The field was large and I fenced it up to begin with, using the same tactics from my old house. But this time, I won't have to spend the night in the field, as I have a comfy place to stay.

Day 8

Now that my field has fences and torches, I can start with the hard work: planting the seeds. But first things first, of course!

I don't have any seeds to work with. The only seeds I had in my house were destroyed along with the chest. And no one has other crops in this village, so I had to find my own seeds in order to start working on my farm.

I grabbed my Shovel and also my Hoe to find some seeds. Wheat seeds are found in tall grass, and you just have to destroy the grass to grab the seeds. As for Melon and Pumpkin seeds, those are really rare and must be found inside chests in dungeons and other places.

But I'll settle with Wheat for now. Wheat can be used to craft Bread and also Cake, and it's the food used to attract other animals. I'm sure Wheat will be really useful for everyone in this village, and I want to show them my appreciation for taking me in.

I found some tall grass and cut it off to find seeds. But the area was short on tall grass, maybe because there were too many trees around. I went even farther, looking for a hill biome where tall grass is more common. Luckily, there was a grassy hill next to the jungle where I found plenty of seeds to start my farm.

Then I returned to the fields and used my Hoe to plow the land. I planted the seeds, one next to the other, and the farm was getting in shape. Now I just had to wait for the first crops to come out, and maybe use some bones to grow them faster.

Bones aren't easy to find, because they're only dropped by Skeletons. And Skeletons are dangerous… Maybe it's just easier to wait for the crops to grow on their own.

Day 9

The first crops were coming out nicely. As a farmer, it made me really happy to grow my crops after working so hard on them.

As the crops grew, I had nothing else to do, so I decided to stop by the village and visit the other residents. I wanted to talk to them and know what they were working with. Joseph took me on a small tour to see the other workers.

"We've got miners, builders, crafters, priests, architects, store owners, guards, everything. This village is full of skilled people who are proud of their jobs." Joseph said.

"That's outstanding. I like to do my job as a farmer too." I said.

"And you should be! Everyone in the village is eager to receive some of your Wheat once you are done. Wheat is a rare ingredient and it's hard to cultivate, but now that we have a farmer here who's specialized on it, everyone wants some."

"Really? I know Wheat is a good ingredient for many things, but I didn't know it was that popular."

"You can bet it is!" Joseph said. "Wheat is formidable. Everyone is anxiously waiting for your new crops. And oh, by the way, the other citizens are willing to exchange their resources with you for the Wheat!"

"How does that work?" I asked him.

"It's simple. Everyone produces something, be a product or a service. We exchange these goods for others, it's a mutual trade. That's how we keep things running here. In other words, you can trade your Wheat for other goods or services, or you can simply sell it to a store."

"That's really clever."

"Yes, the system works just fine. Here, let's go visit the other workers. They want to give you something." Joseph said.

We visited other players and everyone shared some of their own goods with me. I got a lot of Iron, Gold, Diamond, Melons, Tools and Weapons, Armor pieces, and even a Map. In the end, we visited the guards and they had a few items taken from the monsters. They gave me some bones and arrows, and now I could grow the crops using bones.

I have no words to express how thankful I am for living here. The residents of this humble village work hard every day and even so, they're happy to offer me their items. I never thought I would find such a nice place. I'm in paradise!

Day 10

Today, I used all of the bones I got from the guards to grow my crops. There was not enough to use in the entire crop, but this will be of great help. Now, I just need to wait for a day to collect everything and I'll be able to distribute Wheat to the other citizens!

I'm so anxious. I can't wait to harvest my first crop in this village. I'll finally be useful for everyone, and Wheat is a product on demand around here. This is a winwin situation for both the residents and me!

Joseph came by to see how I was doing.

"Hey, farmer! How are you going?" He said.

"I'm fine, thanks!" I said.

"Glad to hear that. So, how's the production coming along after receiving all those items?"

"It's really good. Here, check this out! The crops are growing superfast now thanks to the bone meal."

"Very nice. Bone meal grows plants and crops faster; I see the guards were kind to donate some for you."

"Yes, and I am very grateful for that. Now we don't have to wait a week for the crops. In fact, tomorrow everything should be done! I'll harvest and deliver the Wheat to the other citizens, including you."

"Really? Nice job, Mark! If that's the case, I'll stop by tomorrow to help you distribute the Wheat. It will be easier with two people doing it."

"Okay Joseph, I appreciate all of your help. See you tomorrow, then!"

"Alright, see you tomorrow."

The farm will be full of grown Wheat tomorrow, ready for harvest. I'll have a lot of work tomorrow, but this will be a good thing. I'll harvest all the Wheat and everyone in the city will be able to use it as they so desire.

Day 11

What in the world just… happened?!

I woke up today and I went to the farm, anxiously waiting to see the yellow plot of land. But what I witnessed was just a brown plot of land: there was no Wheat there. It was gone.

"What… What happened?!" I thought. "Who did this? Where's all my Wheat?"

I searched the area, trying to find any clues of who could have done such a horrible thing as stealing Wheat from a humble farmer like me. Maybe someone had gotten inside the field

44

when I was asleep? But there were no footsteps in that area…

And who in this village would do that? They're all so gentle and nice; I can't see anyone from this village doing an atrocity like that. I know people wanted Wheat really bad, but not THIS bad, to the point of stealing food from me.

In the afternoon, Joseph stopped by to give me a hand with the production, but there was nothing for us.

"Hey Mark! I'm here to help you today." Joseph said.

"Hey… Joseph, the Wheat…" I said.

"What's wrong, Mark?"

"The Wheat is gone, Joseph! Gone!"

"Gone? What do you mean?"

"It's gone! Someone stole it last night!"

"That can't be." Joseph said, checking the fields. "Someone harvested everything? It was not you?"

"No, I'm telling you. I came here early this morning and the Wheat was gone. like, puff!"

"That's weird, Mark. I mean, the residents of our village are trustworthy friends of ours. They'd never do such a horrendous act as stealing."

"I know Joseph, and I can't argue with that. I trust these people and they've been so nice to me, but someone stole my Wheat. I can't... I can't deliver the production right now. I'm sorry." I said.

"Well, alright then. It's a big shame, everyone was so happy to know that we would have Wheat."

"Yes, I know... I've ruined their plans. And even after everyone offering me their items in exchange for the Wheat... I feel bad for them."

"Don't worry, Mark. I am sure everyone will understand. I'll let them know about the crops, and we can wait until the next one."

"Thanks, Joseph. I appreciate all of your help. I'll go find more seeds now and start all over." I said.

Joseph is being really nice to me. I let him down... Actually, I let everyone down. I really want to compensate the residents for my mistake, and this next crop will be even bigger. I spent the rest of the day looking for seeds, and I got twice as much seeds as before! I planted all of them during the night, working hard until late to repay the residents who have helped me so much.

Day 12

I was working on my farm again on the next day when Joseph stopped by as usual.

"Hey Mark! I see you're working hard. Great job!" He said.

"Thank you, Joseph! I am doing my best. I've been plowing this land all day, and I want to plant more seeds. This crop will be bigger than the previous one. And I'll harvest it, no matter what!"

"Glad to hear it. By the way, I've got some good news for you. Here it is." Joseph said, handing me a pack of bones. "Take these! They'll help you."

"Bones?! Wow! That's a lot of bones! Where did you find them?"

"I told everyone what happened in the farm, and they've been searching around to find the culprit. Also, the guards went after a Skeleton spawner last night and got a load of bones to help you."

"That is so kind of them... Thank you very much! Words can't express my gratitude." I said.

"You're welcome, Mark. Like I said, in this village, we all help each other. And everyone is helping you overcome your problem. I hope those bones fit you just fine."

"They'll improve my production speed by a thousand times. Again, thank you for the help. I'll personally take the Wheat to the other residents when I'm done harvesting everything." I said.

"Glad to hear it! I'm on my way

now; I have to help the miners finish the tracks." Joseph said.

"Okay, bye! See you soon."

They helped me when I first got here and now again. These guys are really kind. If it wasn't for their help, my crop would be growing slowly as days passed by. Fortunately, there's enough bone meal here to grow Wheat until tomorrow.

And then, I shall redeem myself with my friends! I'll give them good and fresh Wheat for their hard work helping me.

Day 13

What in the world? My crops were gone again!

And this time, I even stayed up late to keep an eye out. Everything was just fine, no signs of other humans around, nothing. It was really late and I returned home to take some sleep, and by the morning, the crops were gone.

I don't know what's going on here... I am not even sad anymore, I am angry! My beautiful Wheat, which I planted and cared so much for... Who would steal it from me? This is really bad, I owe these people big time and I can't even pay them back.

Joseph came by the morning.

"Good morning, Joseph! I see you've already taken care of the crops. Nice job!"

"Uh, actually Joseph…" I said. "You won't believe it if I tell you."

"What happened, Mark? Oh… Please don't tell me the crops were taken away again?" Joseph said.

"Unfortunately yes… All gone. I came here this morning, expecting to harvest the crops and take them to the citizens, but it was gone! Seriously, what's wrong with these people? We need to put an end to these thieves!"

"Mark, this is really strange. We haven't had any cases like this in the village so far. No one has stolen anything from other residents, and they've come here for your Wheat. Why would they do that?"

"I don't know Joseph, but someone is behind this. I can tell you for sure, this is another person's doing."

"Alright Mark, we'll look further into this matter. We can't let it continue happening like this. I'll talk to the other residents this afternoon and see if anyone has any ideas. In the meantime, feel free to search for clues or anything that might give us a lead."

"Okay Joseph, I will. Thanks in advance for the help."

Joseph left and I was all by myself on that field. And I simply stood there, staring at the empty field and thinking "Why would someone steal Wheat... Why?"

I am slightly disappointed with this village. I'm not blaming anyone for doing this, but Wheat can't simply disappear on thin air, am I right? I know there must be an explanation behind this occurrence. I just can't seem to find the answer.

Day 14

I returned to the fields, still clueless on what to do next. Should I go look for more seeds? And even if I did, why should I? Unless we find the culprit for stealing Wheat first, there's no point in planting anything right now.

Joseph came to the farm to talk with me.

"Hey Mark, do you have a minute?" He said.

"Sure thing, I was collecting some seeds in the area. What's up?"

"So, can you come with me? The other residents would like to talk to you about the missing Wheat."

"Sure, let's go!" I said.

We walked together and we entered a house atop the tallest tree of the area. Inside, the other residents waited for our return.

"Good afternoon, Mark. I am Sally, one of the builders."

"Hey Sally!" I said.

"According to Joseph, your crops were stolen yesterday once more is that correct?" She said.

"Yes ma'am, I was going to harvest all of the Wheat and when I got there, everything had been harvested already. I don't know who is doing this, but"

"Is there anyone else who

works with you on the fields?" Sally said.

"No, I'm the only one who works as a farmer, as far as I know."

"And have you noticed anything weird in the area recently? Any strange visitors, any other humans that don't live in this village?"

She said.

"No, not at all."

"Then how did it disappear?"

"Good question. I've been asking myself the same thing. I mean, who could have stolen all of my food"

"Mr. Mark, I can assure you no one in this village stole anything from you. I've been living here for years and I know every face and person who is here with us."

"But ma'am, what is this all about? Who could have done it?"

"I'll be frank, Mark. We suspect you are keeping all of the Wheat for yourself."

"What?! But wait, I'm the one who's been suffering the most! I worked so hard to get all the seeds, plant them, and look after the crops..."

"Mark, you are the only person in that vicinity. The other residents donated many items and goods to help you in your job. And I believe you've been taking advantage of our kindness for your own sake."

"No... Lady, I can explain everything. I am not stealing Wheat! I am planting it. And if you guys want your items back, I can give it to you! I promise you, I am not stealing anything."

"Then please, tell me who is

taking all the Wheat, or where this Wheat production is located. If you don't, we'll be forced to remove you from the village."

"But wait, I..."

"You have 24 hours. Everyone is dismissed." Sally said.

57

I climbed down the tree and returned to my house. I have 24 hours to prove I am not a thief! I can't believe this. Why has everything come down to this?! I was living a great life here as a resident, and now I have to prove I am not stealing Wheat for my own benefit.

I must prove I am innocent. I am just a normal player who's striving to get by in this world. I don't want to live all by myself again, and I am not stealing from others. I will have to find a solution somehow, before they throw me out of this village.

Day 15

The day flew by and I had not found a way out. I'm screwed!

Joseph, Sally and other residents came up by my door in the afternoon to ask me for my own version of the facts.

"It's been 24 hours, Mark." Sally said. "What have you got for us?"

"Please Sally, listen to me." I said. "So, I went after all the seeds, I planted them, I looked after the crops... And I was going to harvest them if someone else hadn't stolen them before!"

"And what about the bones you used to produce bone meal?" Sally said. "The guards worked really hard to get those only for you, and this is how you pay them back? With lies?"

"But I am not lying... I promise! Here, let me try this out once more. But this time, I don't want any bone meal or anything. You can take your items back, and I'll even sleep next to the field to make sure no one steals anything. And"

"Enough, Mark. I've seen many liars in my life to know when they're desperate to prove their innocence. Now, you don't have any concrete proof that you're not stealing Wheat. The residents never approached the fields during your time there, and you're the only person working on the crops. What

else?"

"Uh... I know this may sound silly, but please trust me. I am not lying. You just have to trust me!"

"Sorry, Mark. We just can't keep you here anymore. The other residents demand results, and they want the Wheat." Joseph said.

"In this case Mark, you are now expelled from this village." Sally said.

"I am… what?" I asked her.

"Expelled. You've been kicked out. Now please, leave all of the items given to you by the other residents in that chest. And leave this house immediately afterwards, or I'll call the guards."

"Fine, don't worry. I'm leaving peacefully." I said.

I put away my stuff in the chest and left the house. As I walked out of the village, I saw the other residents angrily staring at me.

I left the village and as I walked farther, I tried to realize what went wrong. But it just wasn't clear to me; I had been kicked out for no reason. Now, it was getting dark and I had to find a place to stay before the monsters came out. I holed up in the ground and stayed there for the rest of the night.

Day 16

I woke up today inside a hole. I had been living a nice life in a village with my new friends, and now I have nowhere to go and everyone thinks I am a thief. What a turnaround! I can't even imagine why everything came down to this.

In the morning, I chopped some wood to build myself a small house. I had to do it fast, because I am not good at building things and I don't want to sleep inside a hole once again. The monsters will come out during the night and I must make myself a shelter.

I've been thinking what I did wrong. Why did they kick me out without any valid proof? They couldn't prove I was the one stealing the Wheat and they removed me from the village regardless of my allegations.

That's unfair... I was misjudged by the residents, and now I'm paying the price for something that someone else did. The more I think about it, the angrier I get. Honestly, I have not been this angry before. I'm about to explode!

But this won't end like this... I won't let them get out of this easily. They shall pay for treating me like garbage, and for throwing me out without proving anything. You don't do that with an innocent player.

And I believe I know what I

can do to have my revenge against those residents: I will become a griefer! I've heard tales of griefers before. They are a species of humans who enjoy destroying and causing chaos in other servers.

They don't play the game to have fun with others; they play the game to make fun of people. Most griefers are banned from servers as soon as they are found. But I won't make it easy for anyone. I'll be a shadowy figure, pulling pranks on players and leaving a trace of destruction behind me.

I'll make them regret their decision of banning me without a good reason. Actually, I will make them have a good reason to ban me from this place. And I won't get caught. Just wait for me, you poor village. You won't get away from this! Your punishment is coming.

Day 17

Now that I'm officially a griefer, I need to find out what I can do to cause damage to the village and bother the residents. My main objective here is not to hurt anyone, or to destroy the entire village, but to cause trouble and be a major annoyance. I just want to see them angry and frustrated; I want that perfect mask of theirs to fall off.

First, I must build a house next to the village. But if I don't want them to find me, this house must be hidden somewhere... And I know what I can do. I decided to take down my temporary wooden shelter and use the materials to build a house under the ground.

By doing so, I can ensure no one will ever find me if they decide to go look after me. It will be a good spot to hide and to sleep during the night.

Next, I need to prepare my plans. What am I going to do? How can I disturb their peaceful lives as much as possible? I need to destroy small things. I can also place small traps to annoy them and make them confused.

And I know exactly how I can achieve that: pistons. Pistons are useful items that can be used to create a variety of builds, including traps. By using pistons and pressure plates for these objectives, I'll achieve my main goal with ease.

But I don't have the material needed to build pistons... And that's my main problem. I guess I could enter the village during the night and see if they don't have any pistons in those chests in the main house. Or maybe Iron.

I'll give it a try tonight. I wanna know if I can bypass the guards and enter the village

without being noticed. If I manage to do that, I'm ready to carry on with my next plans, and I can start crafting new traps and other items to place around the village. Be ready, residents! Your peaceful days are almost over.

Day 18

When it was dark and everyone went to sleep, I left my underground hut and headed to the village. I sneaked upon the place and climbed a few trees before reaching it. On top of the tree, I watched the village and tried to find the guards' locations.

I saw at least 6 guards in different areas, and I memorized their area of reach. Their field of view was broad, but if I snuck up on the place from behind, I wouldn't alarm anyone. And I did it – I walked around and entered the village from the back.

Sneaking in was easy. The hard part was getting inside the court house, the one located above the tree, without dragging any attention. Despite not having anyone on the streets at that time, I had to be extremely careful to not alert the guards.

I reached the tree's foot and I looked up. It was a long way of stairs to reach the top, and there were no guards in the region. "This is my chance", I thought. I climbed the stairs and reached the top without too much trouble.

There, I headed to the court house, but the door was locked. I tried to find a way in, but all doors and windows were closed. So I grabbed my pickaxed and opened a 1x2 hole on the wall and entered the court house.

The place was large enough to accommodate all residents, and I looked for the chest room. There was a day I came here with Joseph, but I didn't pay much attention to it. Inside the chest room, I found several items, from armors to minerals and even some TNT.

"TNT? This is like a gift from heavens!" I said.

TNT is the perfect item for the job. It causes massive destruction within a short period of time, and it can even start a big fire if there's wood or cloth nearby. I'll use these TNT blocks as I please, and this village will be in complete chaos when I'm done with my traps.

I also found a lot of Redstone, some Iron, Gold, Slime Balls and even Sticky Pistons. I grabbed everything and quickly left the place. Climbing down the tree was even easier, and I snuck my way out of the village. Success! My mission had been completed

I returned to my base and stored everything in one of the chests I had brought from the court house. I had enough resources to cause mayhem in that village. I may not be the greatest builder, but I sure am a very creative person.

The residents will not even see this coming!

Day 19

In my first day as the new griefer of this world, I wanted to start pulling a classical prank. This is a prank I've heard of from other players and servers, and it is a known tactic by griefers all around the world: the in-house pool.

I grabbed some of the Iron I had and crafted a bunch of buckets. Next, I collected some water from a nearby river and now I just needed to use the shovel to dig a hole inside the resident's house and fill it up with water.

The only purpose of this trap is to annoy. It won't destroy anything or cause any harm, but it will simply be a major annoyance and they'll have to take care of it otherwise the water will not be removed by itself.

I grabbed all buckets and the shovel and went to the village even during the day. Now I had a good plan to infiltrate their place without being noticed. The residents are working during the day, so most houses are empty. It's the perfect time to pull some pranks!

I chose Joseph's house to be the first one. Joseph seemed to be such a nice guy, but in the end he was one of the residents who removed me from the village for nothing. He didn't even have any proof that I was the one who stole the Wheat!

First, I entered the village from the back, like I did the night before. Then I went to Joseph's house. As I expected, no one was home, so I entered the place and grabbed my shovel to dig the hole. After I was done, I filled it up with water. What a sight! A house with a pool of water instead of a floor. I'm sure Joseph will be impressed when he gets here!

But that was not all. I had to include someone else in my priority list: Sally. The other resident who kicked me out of this village. Joseph and Sally will regret kicking me like that! And I did the same thing to her: I filled her house with water.

And these two are not enough. I'll do the same for five other residents, as to keep them distracted as much as possible.

Now that I am done with my pranks, I'll leave the village before someone finds me and wait for the outcome. I'd love to see the look on their face when they return home! Too bad I can't wait here, but I guess I'll stop by tomorrow to see the results.

Day 20

Today, I wanted to go to the village and check things out. I was curious to see the results of my plan, but I could not enter the village like that. So I had to sneak up inside and remain hidden so as not to get caught.

I entered the village from the same place and I headed to Joseph's house first. I heard people inside talking, so I stayed outside next to the window, listening to their conversation.

"I can't even imagine who would do this!" Joseph said.

"This is not funny at all." The other person said. "Whoever did this is probably having a good laugh right now."

"Laugh all they want. I am sure we'll find the one responsible for pulling this prank, Jeff." Joseph said.

"Sure, I'll help you with that. But in the meantime, we need to get all of this water out of here." Jeff said.

"Sure… I heard Sally had the same problem. Other residents informed us they've been trolled too. Y'know, this makes me wonder, why would people do this to us? We're such a friendly village and all."

"I don't know, Joseph. Don't you think it was that guy you kicked out earlier this week?"

"Mark? I don't know. Could be him, but not even the guards spotted anyone coming in and out of the village. Plus, the items from the court house were taken away. This makes me think the person who did this is living here."

"Well, we better watch out. Let's keep an eye out for these incidents before they get out of control." Jeff said.

"Sure. Now, let's dry this place; I can't stand looking at this pool inside my house anymore." Joseph said.

They both worked hard to remove all of the water and close the hole with cobblestone. I quickly left the village and returned to my hut, proud to see the result of my clever prank. Now that I know how to pull the pranks without alerting them, I'll prepare new ones to drive those residents nuts!

Day 21

I returned to the village during the morning. The residents were working as usual, and I took the opportunity to pull my next prank. This is a more elaborate one: I'll put a pressure plate right in front of their doors.

When they enter their house from the main door, a piston system pushes two blocks – one from above and one from below – to close the entrance. They'll have to enter from the back and remove the trap to restore their main entrance.

But that is not all: the moment

they remove the pistons, they'll activate a new trap. There will be two water sources above the roof, and as soon as they remove the piston, the house will be covered in water.

I want to use a lot of water because it slows down the normal movements and it also takes away small items from the house. Water traps are by far one of the most annoying ones, widely used by griefers and trolls all around.

I guess I am more of a troll than a griefer... Or maybe I'm a mix of both. Either way, I am having a lot of fun with this! If I knew that pulling pranks was so much fun, I'd have started doing this a lot earlier.

I chose some random house's to place the traps and started working on them. I didn't have too much time, because I never knew when they would return home from work. But as long as I worked inside the houses, the guards outside would never see me. It was the perfect plan!

And I placed the traps successfully. I'm getting really good at this! Now that the traps are all over, I just have to wait for the results. And once again, I'll be having a good laugh at them while they try to fix everything without knowing who did it. And tomorrow, I'll check things out while also placing new traps around the village.

Day 22

I visited the village and the mood was stranger than usual. The residents were uneasy with the recent events, and rumors started spreading around. I sneaked up to the village and hid inside an empty house, when I overheard two residents passing by.

"Did you hear about what happened to Carl's house?" One of them said.

"I did. The door was closed when he tried to enter, and then his house was filled with some mysterious water!" The other said.

"That's really strange. How did that happen?"

"I don't know man, but I heard one of the residents saying he saw a shadowy figure walking by the village during the day."

"A shadowy figure? What do you mean?"

"I don't know; they're saying there's some kind of ghost wearing a black cape and pulling pranks on people to scare them. Personally, I think that's really scary!"

"Wow, don't even tell me about it. Do you think that ghost could be… Herobrine?"

"Herobrine? That old hoax from the tales? I don't know dude, but no one has seen the creature yet so I guess it could be."

"Well, if it's really Herobrine who's behind all this, we better watch out for any humans with glowing eyes.

I heard Herobrine has very white eyes and can also teleport at will."

"Gee, stop. Now you're scaring me. Anyway, let's go help Victor before it gets dark. He needs some help with his house; it's full of those traps too."

I couldn't believe my ears. My traps worked wonders! Not only they succeeded in irritating and frustrating the humans, but they also created a fake story among the residents. They've been so scared with these random and uncalled pranks, that they think Herobrine did it!

I'm literally laughing right now. They are blaming Herobrine, a hoax that does not even exist, for the traps and the pranks! This is an outcome that I could not predict not even if I wanted. And it is perfect. Now I just need to find white glasses to cover my eyes and I'll be good to scare them to death!

Day 23

I've searched around for something to give me white eyes, and I found a pair of glasses for my skin. I just had to repaint these glasses to white and voilá, the perfect disguise! Now I am officially Herobrine, the scary hoax roaming around the village.

With my newly found identity, I can pull pranks without worrying about getting caught. In case anyone finds me, they'll be scared away by my fake white eyes and I'll continue trolling them without any problems.

Today I grabbed my stuff and

returned to the village. My next prank would be a misdirection. I built several forms across the village using nothing but rock and dirt. Words, shapes, numbers, I built everything I could only using rocks and dirt.

These "abstract forms" are supposed to give them a signal, to let them know there's a living creature behind everything. They don't mean anything; they're just there to further provoke them into thinking that Herobrine really exists.

I've also entered their houses and messed up with their chests. I changed their locations, put in some weird items, filled empty chests with nothing but dirt and sand, and even took out all items and hid them inside the house.

In short, I've been doing everything to drive them insane. The residents haven't had a peaceful day since I started trolling and griefing their village. They're blaming Herobrine for everything, but I'm actually taking advantage of this disguise to continue messing around.

Back to my hut, I spent the rest of the day working on other pranks. I'm trying to elaborate one using pistons and TNT to destroy some houses and chests. Yeah, I wanna get even farther with my pranks and tricks! This is only getting better by the day, and no one can stop me right now.

Day 24

I already had a new plan for the TNT traps. I got some Redstone, Pistons, TNT, Pressure plates, Cobblestone and Levers. With these items, I can pull off several different pranks and tricks causing many explosions inside the village.

I sneaked into the village once again, curious to hear the results from my previous one.

"Man, I can't stand this anymore. I am thinking of leaving this server." I overheard someone saying.

"Me too… I don't want to live in a place haunted by Herobrine."

"I know, right? And Joseph says he will find the person who is doing this. It has been a week and he hasn't found anything. Not even those useless guards can find the one pulling these pranks."

"Like they said, this must be Herobrine. What other person could do everything without getting caught? This is not a normal person's doing."

"You're right. Last night when I came back home, my chest was a mess. I had a chest for food, other for rocks and other for weapons. They were mixed up together and some items were gone. I searched the house and didn't find anything. And the door was locked! How is that possible?"

"Yeah, my chest went crazy too. The items were out of place, and I even found some items that were not mine."

"This is getting out of hand. When does it end? Every day when I return home, I am worried about my own safety. I don't know what kind of trap is waiting for me inside my own house."

"Don't even tell me about it. That's why I want to leave this place. If they don't deal with this quickly, I am out of here."

"Same here. Anyway, see you later."

"See ya."

Perfect. The traps worked! Herobrine is alive more than ever, and it will be hard for Joseph to prove them wrong. As long as I don't get caught, Herobrine will cause even more chaos in this village, and they will never see me coming!

Day 25

With all items at hand, I prepared my new trap inside the village. This trap will be a huge blast... Literally!

It'll be a TNT trap activated by pressure plates. And it is really simple: when the residents step into their houses, they'll activate a pressure plate which triggers a TNT under the ground. The TNT will go off, destroying everything on the ground.

This trap is not dangerous for their own safety, as one TNT underground is not enough to harm a player. But a TNT is capable of destroying a ton of blocks and everything else on its way, including chests and other valuable items.

My main goal here is to cause a massive damage in a short period of time. The purpose of this trap is similar to the one made of water, but the TNT trap is more effective. I sneaked into the village as usual and quickly prepared the trap inside a few houses.

Placing the traps was not hard, but it took me a lot of time. I would not be able to plant the TNT in all houses, so I chose a few to do it. Joseph's and Sally's are among them, of course. I wouldn't let them out of the fun!

But when I was placing the trap inside one of the houses, a person came by from behind and opened the door. He saw me in there, as I was digging the hole to plant the

TNT.

"What's this? Who are you?" He said.

When I turned around and looked at him with my white eyes, the person panicked.

"Oh my god! It's Herobrine! I'm out of here!" He ran away, desperately.

"Haha. These residents are so silly." I thought. "Better keep working and move out of here before others come here to find out who is inside the house."

I finished planting the trap and fled the village. I still had plenty of TNT and pressure plates for other houses, but I had to call it a day. Now to wait for the results. Funny thing is I won't have to come here to check the results. I can literally wait and listen to the results from my house! Hahaha

Day 26

As I expected, last night the residents became agitated. I could hear several explosions from within my underground hut. Ahh, the sweet sound of victory! In the afternoon, I passed by the village to check things out.

Sneaking into the village was harder than usual – everyone was outside today, and no one went to work. The residents spent the day repairing their houses and all the damage caused by the TNT explosions. What a beautiful sight!

"Sir, I am here to inform you that I'll be leaving the village today." One of the residents told Joseph.

"But Peter, come on! I know there's someone out there who is having fun with these pranks, but we can find him! I promise you, we can"

"We can find him? And how? This guy has toying around with us for weeks, leaving traps and all sorts of pranks behind and no one has caught him. Yesterday, one of the residents said he saw the creature inside his house, and it was Herobrine! We can't catch Herobrine."

"For the last time guys, Herobrine does not exist!" Joseph said. "Right, Sally?"

"Correct. Herobrine is just a hoax. He never existed, and he was created by trolls. Whoever is doing this is simply taking advantage of Herobrine's fame to spread rumors. Let's not fall for these mind tricks, please."

"Mind tricks? Does this look like a mind trick to you, ma'am?" One of the residents said, pointing at the houses in pieces.

"I know this is frustrating, but please don't

blame it on an imaginary creature. We need to remain calm during times like these."

"I can't remain calm. Not anymore." The resident said. "My house is gone and I have nowhere to live. My chest was destroyed and I lost many valuable items. I am done. I'm getting out of this village. Good bye and good luck to all of you who stay here." The resident said, walking out of the village.

"In that case, good luck in your future endeavors." Joseph said. "By the way, I'd like to tell everyone that we are not forcing you to stay here. You are free to come and go as you please. But we kindly ask you to stay and help us find the one responsible for the pranks. We'll do our best to help everyone rebuild their houses and even recover their lost items from the chests."

"I need a hand here. My house was destroyed and even the walls are gone."

"Sure, let's rebuild it."

The residents worked all day to repair the damages from the TNT explosions. And I just watched them work hard from far away. My mission has been accomplished!

Day 27

Unfortunately I don't have many TNT blocks left, so I'll have to stop with the TNT traps for now. But that won't be a problem, I've got lava buckets and pistons to help me achieve success!

The village was in a big commotion. Sneaking into the place was possible, but walking around like usual was not. Everyone was outside, helping others rebuild their homes and taking materials in and out.

"Man, this house is a mess! And the explosion came from the

ground, like the others."

"Yeah, this Herobrine guy knows how to pull a decent prank on others."

"He's like a troll and also a griefer at the same time. Scary!"

"Sure is scary. Rumors had it that Herobrine won't stop until everyone has left this place."

"Seriously? Gosh! If things don't stop exploding like that, I might as well leave like the other guy!"

"Same. I won't stay here and play with fire. Herobrine ain't a creature to mess with."

My mind game was working wonders. The residents didn't know who was behind the attacks, and they just called me 'Herobrine' instead. The guards were clueless as well, because they protect the front of the village without realizing I was coming from behind.

This plan can't get more perfect than this, and now I can easily continue with my pranks without ever getting caught. In the end, everyone will leave this village and I will be the winner! You guys kicked me out? Now I am kicking YOU out!

Day 28

I was ready to move onto my next set of traps. I got all of my items and left. But when I went to the village, the entire place had guards all over. They hired new guards and some residents left their old jobs to become guards too.

So they're thinking straight now! That's actually a good thing. I love some challenge! I had to return home and prepare a new plan. I need to find some other way to get inside without getting caught. Maybe underground? Or I could find a blind

spot on their watch.

Either way, it shouldn't be hard sneaking into the village. They're not that good at keeping an eye on invaders, and I'm really good at sneaking in.

Day 29

Today was a crazy day. I didn't wake up in my underground hut – I was inside a white room. Everything was white, even the floor. I felt like I was floating. This room seemed to be completely empty and had no walls, but everything was white. What place is this?

I walked around for a bit, scared with this weird location. And then, I saw someone sitting on a chair in the distance, typing on a computer.

"What the heck? Who is

that?" I asked myself. I approached the person and talked to him.

"Uh… hello? Who are you? Where am I?"

"Oh, so you've finally woken up." The bearded man said. "Nice to meet you. My name is Notch, and you must be Mark."

"Notch… Notch… Wait. THAT Notch?!" I said.

"Yes. I am Notch, the creator of this game. I teleported you to my room here after seeing all the things you've been doing to that poor village."

"Wait… Uh… You know, I was just having fun because they kicked me out of there. I was innocent, I promise!"

"Being innocent of a crime does not give someone the right to punish others. Everyone makes mistakes, and we must correct these mistakes without resorting to violence. Or in this case, griefing and trolling."

"I know, but…"

"No ifs, ands or buts." Notch said. "Now look at yourself in that mirror."

I looked at the mirror next to him and I saw myself using the normal skin and my eyes were completely white.

"What?! What happened to me?"

"From now on, you'll be Herobrine." Notch said.

"Hero... brine? THE Herobrine? Are you kidding me?" I said.

"No. You will be Herobrine for a few weeks. As Herobrine, your duty is to help other players in this world. You'll be assigned several tasks by me and you'll have to fulfill your duty if you want to come back to normal. And if you don't succeed, I will permanently ban you from all servers in this game, meaning you'll be removed forever.

This is your chance to redeem yourself for your mistakes."

"I can't believe this... But why? They're wrong too!"

"They may be wrong, but you're even worse for destroying their properties and pulling pranks. Now, you'll be returned to the world but in a different server. Your duty begins right away. Good luck to your new position as Herobrine, and I'll be around if you have any questions."

Notch disappeared and everything turned white again. And suddenly, I was asleep again.

Day 30

I woke up completely lost. Was that a dream? Or even a nightmare? What happened last night?

But when I stand on my feet, I realized it had not been a dream: I really was Herobrine! I was using the neutral, default skin from the game and I could see my white eyes from the river's reflection. Oh gosh, I am Herobrine and I must help people now!

And how was I supposed to do that? I don't know what I can do to help! I mean, I've been pulling pranks and annoying everyone, I don't know how to do something good for other people...

Then, I saw a book falling from the sky. This purple book had the title "Herobrine's Update" on the main cover, and inside I found the new update introduced to the game. The update had the following:

Patch notes for the Herobrine Update

Added new mob: Herobrine; He has permanent glossy white eyes

Herobrine can't craft anything on his own, but he can remove and place blocks and can carry items and use tools

Herobrine can speak with other players, but he cannot lie

Herobrine will be randomly assigned to worlds in need of help

Herobrine can take damage from both humans and monsters, but his presence does not attract monster; His health pool is larger than regular humans

Herobrine will be removed from the game in 6 months if he doesn't fulfill his duty

Note: If you have any doubts, contact me.
Notch

Oh my gosh... This can't be real!

Day 31

Now that I've become Herobrine, I don't know what I must do. I am completely lost and I don't even know where to start. Notch said I must fulfill my duty as the Herobrine by helping others in need.

I didn't know Herobrine was actually a good creature, who helped new players and others who needed him. But what's even worse is that I've used Herobrine's reputation to my advantage as a griefer, and now everyone thinks Herobrine is a monster who destroys houses and

griefs worlds!

This won't be easy. I don't know what to do, but I can't stop now. If I don't complete my mission, I will be banned forever, and I don't want that! I just want to go back to normal... I just want to have a normal life!

I need to prove myself to Notch. And this won't end until I do the opposite of what I've been doing so far!

Book 2: Punished

Day 1

A month ago, I was a normal player who was living in a brand new server and trying to get by. I managed to find a village where other players invited me to live with them. Everything was going great until the day I was accused of stealing Wheat, and was kicked out of the village.

Infuriated with their decision, I began trolling and griefing the villagers to get my revenge on them. And now, Notch, the game developer, has made me pay for my crimes. I've become Herobrine to

help citizens who are in dire need.

What am I supposed to do as Herobrine?! Everyone hates the name Herobrine and it scares everyone away. And now I need to help others to get back to normal? This is insane! I don't know why Notch has done this to me or what he wants me to accomplish, but this is simply crazy.

I guess I don't have much of a choice... I should just get over with this as soon as possible, before I get permanently banned from all servers!

Day 2

Well, well... I must say, being Herobrine feels weird. I mean, I never dreamed of becoming Herobrine, but one might think it must be super cool to be him. And I gotta say, it is not. Being Herobrine is super lame... And boring!

I can't do anything I want, and I can't choose where to go. Notch spawned me in a different server from the one where I was living, because right now I am in the middle of snowy tundra and I don't know where I need to go! Notch just said "help others", but I don't see anyone around here.

And how can I help them? If these Patch Notes are true, I can't craft items anymore, and I can't lie when speaking to others. This will be hard. I've been deceiving and tricking everyone for a month, and now I must act like a goody twoshoes towards others.

Well, I can't waste too much time here. I should look after other humans who could be living in this world. I don't know where they are or what kind of help they need, but just sitting here doing nothing won't help my cause. After all, I don't want to get permanently banned!

Day 3

I've been wandering around in this strange world... What a pain. This is nothing but an empty world filled with trees and snow. Where's everyone? Where's the help they need? I guess Notch sent me to the wrong world, because this place is boring.

Let's see... So I can't craft anything but I can place and remove blocks, I can't lie, and I can even use tools. These rules sure are tough; it means I'll need to work along with other humans if I want to succeed in

my main goal to help others.

But my only problem is I don't have anyone to help! This is a snowy world and it's completely empty. Where should I go next? Does Herobrine have any special powers to locate other players or something?

And when I was about to give up and find a cave to stay during the night, I saw a small wooden house in the middle of the snow. A house built by a player! Finally, now I can help someone and get rid of this punishment once and for all.

But wait… I'm Herobrine! I am not a normal player anymore. What if I show up on their front door and they get scared? I can't just say "Hello there, I'm Herobrine and I am here to help you".

I can't believe I am now paying for what I did. I've abused Herobrine's reputation as a griefer, and most players don't trust or like to hear the name Herobrine. I can't lie and say I am another person, and I must help them… What now?

For the time being, I've decided to remain hidden and observe. I want to know how

many people live in that house, who they are and what they are doing. That's the only thing I can do right now.

Day 4

Here's my report of my first day observing the house: I saw one human player coming out of the house, only once. Apparently he is a man and we are probably of the same age. I can't tell if there's another person living there with him.

It's not clear yet why he needs help. His house looks good, and he looks safe. Maybe I don't have any other choice than to approach the human and try to convince him that I am here to offer my help.

"This is it." I thought. "Let's do it!"

I walked towards the house and knocked on the door.

"I'm coming!" I heard someone saying.

I was feeling really nervous. I was probably more nervous than the person who was about to meet me outside of his house. When the person opened the door, I said:

"Uh, excuse me, I am Herobrine and I am here to help you…"

"Herobrine? Oh, I think I've heard of you before." The player said. "My name is Ned. Please, come in! It must be really cold outside."

"Oh… Sure, thank you." I said, confused by his hospitality.

"Would you like a cup of tea?" He said.

"No, I'm good, thank you." I said. "Er, anyway. I'm here to offer you my help. There must me something you need help with, correct?"

"Yes! How did you know?" He said.

"Well… My Herobrine powers told me…" I said. "*I didn't want to say that!*" I thought.

"Ah, interesting. Well, I've tamed a horse a while ago but now he disappeared. I don't know where he went, but I'd appreciate it if we could find him. His name is Leonard."

"A horse? Alright… I will try to find him for you." I said.

"Really? Thank you very much!"

"No worries." I said. And now, I had to find a horse for my very first task as the Herobrine.

Day 5

I've left Ned's house and now I'm on my way to find his horse. It's been snowing a lot lately and Ned could not leave his house to look for his horse, but strange enough I don't feel cold. Maybe this is one of Herobrine's perks after all.

I searched the area next to his house, but the horse was nowhere to be found. Then, I amplified the search area to a wider range. I walked south first and then headed east, then north and west. By the end of the day, I had walked a few miles and still

no signs of his horse.

I guess I'll give it a try tomorrow. I can't see anything during the night, and the horse can't be that far. What's really strange is how Ned wasn't scared of my presence. He greeted me as if I was a normal player, and even said he had heard of Herobrine before.

What does that mean? Is he such a new player that he has never heard of the old tales regarding Herobrine, or how scary Herobrine is supposed to be? Either way, I'm glad he didn't run away when I talked to him.

This makes my job easier, and I don't have to do anything else other than find his horse for him. Oh, speaking of which… where did that horse go?!

Day 6

Another day searching for the missing horse in the snowy plains. The white forest makes it extra difficult to search for anything, let alone a horse that can easily hide behind a tree or something. Being Herobrine ain't easy...

I looked for the horse everywhere. I didn't know what else I could do, so I remembered what the patch notes said: I should contact Notch when I had a doubt! But how exactly could I contact him?

"Notch, if you are there,

please listen to me. I really want to talk to you." I said out loud.

"What do you need help with, my friend?" Notch said, standing by my side.

"Woah there! You scared me for a moment!" I said. "How did you appear next to me so fast?"

"By teleporting, duh. I have Admin rights in every single server in this world. So, do you need my help or not?"

"In fact, I do. You assigned me to this world and I'm supposed to find a horse. But I have not found it yet, and I can't seem to be lucky today…"

"Hmmm, finding an animal, huh." Notch said. "Very well. I should grant you one more power. Just a minute, I'll update your patch notes and you'll be able to find any animal with ease."

Notch disappeared for a brief moment and returned with a new purple book.

"There you go. I've updated your patch notes. You know have an extra skill."

"An extra… skill?" I asked him.

"Yeah. Check out your book." Notch said.

I opened the purple book and read the new patch notes:

Patch Note 1.01

Updated skills: Herobrine can talk to animals.
This skill serves for neutral and nonhostile animals, not hostile mobs.

"Wait… Now I can talk to animals?!" I asked Notch.

"Yes. I'm really curious to

know how you'll put that skill to use. I want to know how this will impact your decisions in order to help others."

"But… why? Why are you doing this? Giving me special skills, the

126

ability to talk to animals and everything…"

"Because you're being tested. I am evaluating not only your condition as a human, but also as someone who must prove himself as worthy of playing on these servers. I want to see how your skills will help others, and by others I am not only talking about humans."

"Not only about humans? What does that mean?"

"Farewell. I've already helped you today. Now go on and look for the horse." Notch said.

"But, I still need some help!" I said, as Notch disappeared into thin air.

"Ah… Well, I have no idea how this will help me with my quest, but I guess it's better than nothing." I thought.

And with my brand new ability, I tried to find the horse once again, and I failed once more. Where the heck are you, little horse?

Day 7

Now that I can speak with animals, I used my new skill to call for the horse. I called for him in the woods and in the plains, hoping that he would answer my call, but didn't get any response.

"Where are you, horse? Come on, your owner is worried about you!" I said.

As I walked further into the woods, the horse finally came out.

"Ah, there you are! I've been looking for you for days!" I said.

"Wow... I can actually understand what you're saying." The horse said.

"I know that. I have the ability to talk to animals!" I said. "Nice to meet you, my name is Herobrine. I'm here to take you back to your owner. He's been very worried with you."

"Oh, I got it. He sent you after me, didn't he?" The horse said. "Sorry but I don't want to go back anymore."

"Pardon?" I said. "And why not? He's been asking for you all the time!"

"Sorry, but my owner is a bad owner. He doesn't take care of me properly. He rarely feeds me, and he lets me sleep outside, where it is extremely cold."

"Oh, really? I didn't know that…" I said.

"Well, did you see any stable there? It's only his house." The horse said.

"Now that you said it, it's true. I should have noticed that before… He had a horse, but there was only one house in there. There wasn't a stable."

"Yes. I've been living with him for a while

now, but he doesn't know how to take care of a horse. What's even worse, I can't communicate with him because he is a human. So I'd rather live here in the woods than live with him again."

"I understand you horse, but I think I know how to deal this situation. So please, come back with me and we'll talk with Ned. Maybe we can find a solution that is beneficial for all parties."

"Alright then Herobrine, I

will trust you because you can speak with me." The horse said. "Hop on my back, we'll get there faster."

"Really?"

"Sure, I'm a horse! I like to ride and run really fast."

"Okay then, let's go!"

Day 8

Back in Ned's house, I talked with him about the horse and how to properly train and take care of him.

"My horse is back! Thank goodness." Ned said. "Thank you for taking him back, Mr. Herobrine!"

"My, my." I said. "I suppose you're a new player in this server for thanking Herobrine so cheerfully without being scared by me."

"Ah yes, I am a new player 'round here! I just got used to this survival thing."

"Yes, I figured. And you know why? Because you haven't been taking care of your horse as you should."

"Excuse me? What do you mean?"

"Your horse needs to be fed, and he needs a good and warm place to sleep during the night."

"Oh, I thought he could simply eat grass and all that." Ned said.

"No, you must feed Wheat or Carrot to your horse. He will be hungry if you don't! Plus, food restores his health packs whenever he gets hurt by any hostile mob."

"That's something I didn't know, sorry about it."

"And make sure you get him a nice place to stay during the night, or he'll have to sleep under the cold snow."

"Sure, I'll build him a stable! That should do it, right?"

"Hmm, sounds good. Thanks for the help, Herobrine!" the horse said.

"It's my pleasure to help, horse. I'm happy to know you two are together. Now, if you

excuse me, I must go."

"Really? And where are you going?" Ned said.

"To be really honest, I have no idea. Probably somewhere else where there are people in need."

"Cool! Good luck with your next quests!" Ned said.

"Thank you. I guess I'll need it…" I said.

Day 9

Today I woke up inside the white room again. Notch was sitting by his desk, typing on his computer.

"Ah, there you go." Notch said. "Finally up. Are you feeling alright?"

"Yes, just a bit… dizzy." I said.

"Sorry. Just a little side effect of the teleports, but it will pass. Anyway, congratulations on your first quest."

"So you saw everything?" I said.

"Sure. That's also why I granted you the ability to speak with animals."

"You wanted me to take the best decision based not only on what Ned had to say, but also on what the horse had to say, right?"

"Correct. It's always important to notice that for every story there are two versions. We should not support one side without looking at the other. You've successfully taken the best decision to help both sides, and I'm happy to see you're doing really good as Herobrine."

"Thank you, I'm trying my best." I said. "What's the next step, Notch?"

"For your next quest, I have something new for you. I'll teleport you to another world, where you'll

have to help a person in need."

"Okay… I'll do my best to help them."

"I'm sure you will, Mark. Now, please take a sit and relax. I'll teleport you as soon as you've recovered your senses. You'll wake up in this other server and then you can proceed to complete your quest. Good luck, and see you soon." Notch said.

I closed my eyes, took a deep breath and relaxed. Then, I just blacked out.

Day 10

I woke up today in a different world. This time, I was no longer in the snow. This world was sunny and covered with green forests, unlike the previous one.

"Alright, time to get moving. I need to find my next client." I said.

This time around, Notch was kind enough to teleport me not too far from my objective – A few minutes after walking and I ran into the cobblestone house built by a player. I innocently knocked at the door and waited for the person to

come out.

"Oh, a visitor? I'll be there shortly." I heard someone saying inside the house.

But in my innocence, I totally forgot I was Herobrine. And that not all players in this world are new players who have never heard of Herobrine, like Ned.

When the man opened the door and saw me, he almost ran away in fear.

"Hello sir, I am Hero"

"HEROBRINE! Oh my gosh, run for your lives!" He slammed the door on my face and ran inside the house.

"Ah... I should've anticipated this." I thought.

But it was too late – I had already scared the man, and gaining his trust would not be easy. Herobrine's fame is bad on different servers, and becoming Herobrine is a hard task.

I tried to talk him down out of it, but it was pointless. The man would not respond to my inquiries. Despite my efforts, he refused to come out of the house and listen to what I had to say.

"But sir, I am here to help you." I said at the entrance.

"Just please, go away! I don't want you to ruin my life! Please go!"

I left the house and returned to the woods. It was better to leave him like that. I'll try to talk with him when he has calmed down a bit.

Day 11

I waited an entire day to talk with the man once again. I observed him from the woods, and he seemed to be very cautious about everything. He stayed inside his house all day and every now and then, he would come out of the door, take a look outside and go back in.

"Sigh. How am I supposed to approach him now?" I thought.

I watched the man and tried to think of a new way to talk with him. I should try to find out about his likes, his dislikes, something that could give me an advantage to start a conversation or a dialogue.

Man, being Herobrine ain't' as easy as I originally thought. Things went so smooth with Ned, that I had completely forgotten how terrifying Herobrine could be. The mere presence of Herobrine is enough to scare away any player in sight.

Well, I can't fight against that. Herobrine's popularity has increased throughout the years, and many griefers and trolls have taken advantage of this hoax to boost their pranks. Yes, myself included. Shame on me...

Anyway, I'll keep an eye out for the man. I need to talk with him. There must be something he needs help with, and I will try to help him to achieve my objective. Let's see if I can discover anything else.

Day 12

Another day, and nothing new so far. The man seems to be as scared as always, and doesn't come out of his house. I can no longer just wait here... He won't give up. I must go there and try to talk to him.

I stepped out of the bushes and was heading towards his house when I heard footsteps coming from the woods. More humans? I quickly hid behind the trees and watched my surroundings.

I saw a group of four humans heading to the man's house. They knocked on the door and he came out.

"Hello Parker, how have you been?" One of the four men said.

"II'm great, thank you." Parker said.

"So, what do you have for us?"

"SSorry Richard, I don't have the minerals to pay for my debt... "

"What do you mean with you don't have the minerals? Come on Parker, you're letting me down. I've given you several chances to prove yourself and to pay for the land you're using here on my server, and you just ignore my kindness?"

"NNo sir, I am not ignoring your kindness. In fact, I am truly glad for everything you've done for me!" Parker said.

"I can see that. You've been

having a good time without having to pay anything for it!" Richard said.

"BBut sir..."

"No ifs and buts, Parker." Richard said. "My guards and I will come back in a few days and you better have my minerals, or we're kicking you out of this server."

"But sir, I only have two gold ingots... I can give those if you need it!"

"Two?! Pff. Don't make me laugh, Parker! Two gold ingots are not enough to pay for your fees. Now, I'll give you a few more days because I am a kind human being. You better have my ten Diamonds when I come back."

"Ten Diamonds?! II thought you only need eight..."

"Yeah. Eight Diamonds plus two more for making me wait. I'll be back soon, Parker! Get to work!" Richard said, leaving the house with his guards.

"I can't... I can't mine so many Diamonds in just a few days... I don't want to get kicked out of here!" Parker said.

I watched everything from the woods. So that's why Parker seemed to be scared with everything. Well of course, I scared him even more, but he had his reasons to be afraid. I need to help him somehow.

Day 13

Today, I tried to talk with Parker again. After listening to his conversation with the other humans, I was more confident on convincing him to believe me.

I knocked on the door and called for him.

"Parker? Are you in there? It's me again, Herobrine."

"Oh gosh, go away!" Parker said. "And how did you know my name?! Just leave me alone! You're Herobrine, I bet you'll destroy

everything here!"

"No, you've got it wrong Parker." I said. "I listened to your conversation with Richard yesterday. I know everything."

"So what? It's none of your business!"

"Parker, open the door so I can help you. I know you are in need. Listen, I am Herobrine but I am not a bad person. I've been helping others and I am here to assist you as well. I want to help you find the Diamonds you need to pay your debt with Richard, so you can live a peaceful life here without them harassing you. Trust me, I am a good person."

Parker slowly opened the door and peeked through it.

"Are you willing to help me?"

"Of course. I am here to help. Just tell me how I can help you."

"Alright... II'll trust you, Mr. Herobrine." Parker opened the door and invited me to his house. "PPlease come in... It's a simple house, but it's mine. I built it when I arrived in this server."

"This place looks really nice." I said.

"Thanks. Uh... It's weird to talk with the Herobrine."

"And why's that?" I said.

"I don't know... I always thought Herobrine was a scary creature who liked to explode things and drive people crazy... Like a troll..."

"Unfortunately, bad players use Herobrine's name to make fun of others. I am not a bad person, and I am trying to clean my name by helping others."

"Oh... Okay. WWell... I came to this server a few months ago and Richard, the admin, was very nice to me in the beginning. He gave me this area to live and let me build whatever I want. But as time passed, he charged me for living here, and I had to pay 5 Diamonds a month as a fee. This monthly fee increased to 6, 7 and 8 and now he's asking for 10 Diamonds."

"Hmm, so he's been asking for money in exchange to let you live here?"

"Yes… And I can't find 10 Diamonds that easily… They're very rare in this world, and I don't have the skills to find so many… Even worse, I don't have decent tools or armor, since all of my valuable minerals goes to Richard to pay for my fees…"

"This is really unfair, Parker." I said. "No one should be charged to live in this world. This place is big enough to accommodate every single human and there would be plenty of empty space to build anything."

"I know but… I don't have other servers to play on."

"Alright. Don't worry; I'm sure we'll find a solution for this problem." I said

I really hope I do... Notch is watching me after all.

Day 14

Decided to learn more of Parker's routine, I followed him into the mines to see for myself what were the chances of finding Diamonds in that server. The server had their own mines, divided in several tunnels and sections, and Parker was assigned to one of those sections.

"I can only mine in the 56th section." Parker said.

"But why? Gosh, look at this world! It's so huge, and yet you're tied to only a small tunnel?"

"Yes… I can't choose where to mine. I can't dig any holes without the owner's permission. This is my limitation."

"This server is really bad… I really think you should go find a different one. But anyway, if you want to stay here, we'll fix this place up."

We went to the mine and I saw other players mining their own sections.

"The others live in specific areas too, and everyone is assigned to a different section of the mine."

"Does everyone around here must pay the fee?" I asked Parker.

"Yes. Everyone here must pay Richard, and we must do it by the end of the month."

We passed by a few miners and Parker greeted them.

"Oh hey John." Parker said.

"Howdy, Parker. Ready for another day of hard work?"

"Yeah… I suppose."

"And who's your friend with the white eyes?"

"He is uh…. Herobrine…"

"Herobrine? Haha. That's funny. Nice skin, bro! Anyway, good luck with the mining. I still need to find 3 Diamonds to pay my debt. What about you?"

"Uh… I need to find 10…"

"10? Wow, that's a lot."

"Yeah… I gotta get to work before they kick me out of here." Parker said.

I followed him into the mine and I observed the section where he worked.

"So this is the place?" I asked him.

"Yeah... This is where I must find the Diamonds..."

"But this place doesn't look really good. How many Diamonds have you found so far in this section?"

"I rarely ever find 5 Diamonds a month."

"A month? Gee, that's not enough!" I said.

"Back in my days, I could find 5 Diamonds in a single day."

"Really? How?" Parker asked me.

"By mining everywhere. Once you're in the correct height, just mine to different sides and eventually, you'll run into the Diamonds!"

"But... I can't do that here."

Parker said. "If I mined in places other than my own section, Richard would get angry at me."

"I think Richard is slowing you down on purpose. All of you. This is slave work, you just work to supply his demand for Diamonds and to pay for a land that should be free for everyone. This is unfair." I said.

"I know… But what else can we do?"

"I think I know what to do. Let's go back to your house." I said.

Day 15

Back in Parker's house, I told him to take me to Richards' house, or wherever he lived in. I wanted to talk to him in person.

"But Herobrine... He will get mad at you for telling him that."

"It doesn't matter, Parker. This must be said. Richard must know he is mistreating everyone in this server, and that he should stop doing so."

"Okay. I will take you there."

Parker said.

We walked up the hill and followed the cobblestone trail leading to Richard's house. Better yet, Richard's temple. He lived in a fancy temple, while everyone else who worked really hard to pay him lived in simple houses.

Richard was inside, sitting on his throne, surrounded by guards.

"Who's this?" Richard asked me.

"Richard, I am Herobrine and I'd like to talk to you."

"Herobrine? The legend? Don't make me laugh. Now take off that fake skin and go back to work." Richard said.

"I don't live here, Richard. I am Parker's friend."

"Oh really? Then you better pay 2 Diamonds for visiting my server. Or get out and don't come back."

"That's why I want to talk to you. You've been stealing Diamonds from these players. That's unfair; they should not pay for a free land."

"Free land?! Who do you think covers the costs for the server and everything else?" Richard said.

"Herobrine, llet's go back home..." Parker said.

"No, Parker! This guy needs to learn his lesson. He must stop right away!"

"Enough with your chitchat." Richard said. "Guards, arrest him."

Arrest me? I am Herobrine! You can't arrest me!"

The guards grabbed me and put me in jail.

"Now stay there until we ban you from the server. And Parker, go back to your house immediately before I raise your fee to 15 Diamonds."

"Yes sir, sorry! Sorry, Herobrine! I must go…" Parker said.

"Don't worry, Parker. Don't get in trouble because of me. Go home, I'll figure this out." I said from the cell.

Parker returned home and I stayed there in the prison. Now what? I may be Herobrine, but I am still a physical creature with limited capabilities. Plus, I can't craft or lie... It will be hard to get out of this mess.

Day 16

Now that I was in jail, I had to find a way out. Unable to lie or to craft anything to take me out of there, I had to resort to another option: I called Notch.

"Notch, can you hear me? I'd like some help here, please." I said.

"Have you called me?" Notch said behind my back.

"Woah, that was fast!" I said. "Notch, I need some help. These guys are harassing other players on this server and they've locked me up in this cell. Can't you do anything about it?

You're Notch! You have access to all servers!"

"As the game's developer, my main duty is to keep it running smoothly for everyone, with constant updates and patches fixing all minor errors and adding new features to the servers. Of course I can't simply ignore what griefers and trolls do, but that's why I select people like you to do that job."

"What? So I'm not the only one who's become Herobrine to help other people?"

"No. Many others have taken the role too. And now, it's your turn to prove yourself as a good player and pay for your mistakes as a griefer."

"Alright… Then, how do I get out of here? Can you grant me a new skill or something?"

"Let's see… Well, I could give you a new ability. But this would make things too easy for you. Come on; try to get out of this situation by yourself. Use the skills you already have and convince the player to stop harassing others."

"But I can't... He doesn't even believe I am Herobrine."

"Very well, then prove it!" Notch said.

"Prove it? How so?" I said.

"You'll figure it out. Anyway, I have already updated your abilities once, now I can only give you two new updates when needed. If I were you, I'd save them for later; Trust me, you'll need it."

"Uh... Okay. I'll see what I can do."

"Sure, I'm counting on you. Good luck, Herobrine." And Notch disappeared.

I don't know what he means with "you'll need it", but I must focus on my mission.

Day 17

The guards passed by my cell and I asked them for Richard.

"Hey there, can I speak to Richard? It's very important." I said.

"What do you want, Herobrineskin?" The guard said.

"I want to prove I am actually Herobrine, and that you are making a mistake for locking me up in here."

"Ha! Richard does not have time to waste with people like you."

"Please, just tell him I can prove I am Herobrine if needed. I am sure he'll be curious enough to come see me."

"Whatever, dude. I'll talk to him later." The guard said.

In the afternoon, Richard stopped by for a visit.

"So, the guard told me you want to prove yourself as Herobrine?" Richard said. "That's impossible, kid!"

"No, it's not. I have some unique skills and I can show you if you want."

"Unique skills? Yeah, like you could have that. What kind of skills?"

"I can speak with animals." I said.

"What? Don't make me laugh! That is a total lie."

"No, it is not because I can't lie."

"Okay! I'll bite the bait. Let me bring you one of my dogs and let's see if you can talk with him! Guards, bring Rex here!" Richard said.

The guard went after the dog and brought him to the prison.

"Now, speak with him and tell me what he has to say!" Richard said.

"Hello, Rex. I am Herobrine. How are you doing?"

"Herobrine? I can understand you... Why is that?" The dog said.

"Because I can speak with animals. So tell me Rex, how's life here in this temple, or castle, or whatever it is?"

"It's a castle!" Richard said.

"Whatever..." I said.

"Life's good. I can't complain really, I like my owner." Rex said. "But it's strange how he treats other humans... I don't know why he does that."

"Me neither, Rex." I said. "But can you tell me what he does with those Diamonds he's getting?"

"Diamonds? You mean those weird rocks?"

"Yes, the blue gems given by the other players." I said.

"Blue? What is that?" Rex said.

"Oh right... Dogs can't see colors. My bad."

"He uses the rocks to craft items and weapons, that's all I guess." Rex said.

"And can you tell me where he keeps those rocks?"

"He keeps them inside a hidden room in the roof of his castle."

"Look at that, he's really trying to talk with Rex! This guy is crazy!" Richard said.

"No, I am not crazy. Rex told me you keep all Diamonds in a hidden room inside the roof of your castle, is that true?" I asked him.

"What... How did you find out? I've never told anyone about it!" Richard said.

"Richard, I can speak with animals." I said.

"I can listen to what they have to say. Is that enough of a proof that I am Herobrine?"

"No... That can't be... That could be a trick. I am not convinced yet!" Richard said.

"No worries. I can prove to

you with my other abilities." I said.

"Sir, we have a problem." One of the guards said.

"What is it?" Richard said.

"The hordes... Somehow, the frontline has been taken over." The guard said.

"What?! Again? I can't believe this... Enough with this chitchat, Herobrine! I've got other important business to deal with." Richard said, leaving me in the cell.

"But wait! Let me out of here!" I said.

Richard and the guards left the prison because there was an emergency. What was it all about?

Day 18

Richard came to the prison with the guards.

"Come on Herobrine, we are taking you out of here!" He said.

"Oh finally!" I said.

"No, we're not releasing you! We are taking you to another place. This area will be surrounded by monsters tonight." Richard said.

"Oh? Why's that?" I said.

"We don't know. The monsters have been attacking our region for many months. We've tried to hold them off as much as we could, but they managed to get past our defenses. And I had a bunch of guards armed to the teeth with Diamond weapons…"

"So that's where you're using your Diamonds?" I said.

"Yes!" Richard said. "I have been using all Diamonds to protect the players and help this community. See how good of a person I am?"

"No, you are not good. You are a selfish and arrogant person who's trying to manage this server by controlling everyone." I said.

"I don't have time to waste with you! Come on, we need to go to the shelter." Richard said.

"Sir, the monsters are already coming out of the spawner." The guard said.

"Now?! It's still daytime!"

"We know, but there are too many of them…"

"Wait. Did you say a spawner?" I said.

"Yes, there are 3 spawners to the south that are always spawning new monsters, we've tried to destroy them but everytime we get close, a hundred mobs come right at us." Richard said.

"Okay. So here's the deal, I destroy the three spawners for you and you stop being such an arrogant leader. Better yet, you'll have to resign from your position." I said.

"What?! Are you mad? I am not gonna do that! Like you could destroy the spawners, haha!"

"Well, I didn't say anything but that's also one of my abilities as Herobrine. The monsters don't attack me. I can easily enter the area and destroy the spawners without a single scratch."

"Nah, you're just lying to me. Let's go to the shelter!" Richard said.

We all went to the shelter, which was an underground bunker. All other players were inside, waiting for us.

"Herobrine, good to see you!" Parker said.

"Hey, Parker! Long time no see." I said.

"So, aare you worried with the monsters? Because I sure am…" Parker said.

"Don't be, Parker. I will deal with the monsters, when Richard stops being stubborn." I said.

We stayed inside the bunker during the night.

Day 19

No one knew how bad things were outside. And the guards decided to check it out in the morning.

"Sir, we just peeked outside and the place is full of Creepers and Spiders." The guard said.

"Gosh. Why won't they go away?" Richard said.

"They're immune to the sunlight, unlike Zombies and Skeletons." The guard said.

"Sigh. I guess we'll have to stay here a bit longer." Richard said.

"Or I could deal with this situation if you stopped being so stubborn." I said.

"Stop bothering me, dude. You can't do anything. You're just lying to me." Richard said.

"No. I can help you and everyone in this server, but you're

denying them the right to have a free life. Now, I will go out, destroy those three spawners and take care of the remaining Spiders and Creepers. I just need a Diamond Pickaxe and Sword because I can't craft anything. Either you accept my terms and hand out your title, or deal with the consequences and let the monsters destroy the place. It's up to you." I said.

"Sir... I think you should reconsider." The guard said. "By tomorrow morning, more Creepers and Spiders will have spawned from the spawners, and will be wandering around the houses. The longer we wait to take action, the worse it gets. If we try to go heads on with the Creepers, we'll end up destroying most of the place because of their destruction. If this guy can do what he says, then we're safe."

"Sigh. I don't have any other choice, do I?" Richard said. "Very well. I, hereby declare that I am no longer the leader of this server. Satisfied?" Richard said.

"Yes." I said. "My Diamond Pickaxe and Sword, please."

"There you go." The guard said, giving me the sword and the pickaxe.

"Alright. I will be back shortly!" I said.

"Good luck out there, Herobrine!" Parker said.

They opened the vault door and I left the bunker. The guards and Richard peeked from the door as I walked past the monsters without disturbing them.

"How the heck does he do that?!" I heard Richard saying. "The monsters are not after him!"

"He really must be Herobrine after all, sir!" The guard said.

I went straight to the area where the spawners were. I found three spawners, two Creepers' and one

Spider spawner. I destroyed them using the pickaxe and proceeded to slay the monsters, one by one.

This was relatively easy because the Diamond Sword was strong enough to take them down in one hit, not giving the monsters time to react. The players watched me slay all creatures from the bunker. Richard couldn't believe his eyes, because he realized I have been telling him the truth all this time.

I returned to the bunker 30 minutes later and told everyone to come out.

"The area is clear. You're free to go now." I said.

"Thank you, Herobrine. We've been saved by you." The guard said.

"As for you, Richard." I said.

"Yes?" He said.

"Never, ever again mistreat other players. If you do that again, I will come back here to deal with you. This is a friendly warning." I said.

"Okay, alright! You win. I promise I won't do anything again! Just don't hurt me, Herobrine!"

Richard said.

"I won't hurt you. And as for the next leader, I believe Parker suits the role just fine."

"Me?!" Parker said. "But why?"

"You are a generous and honest player, Parker. You may be timid, but this should not be taken as a bad trait. Just make the right thing for everyone and you'll be a popular leader among your friends."

"Thank you, Herobrine! I am honored to be chosen by you. And I will do my best for the server!"

The server was back to normal. Richard was no longer the dictator in the place and the monster spawners had been destroyed.

Day 20

I woke up once again in the white room.

"Ah, so I suppose I completed my mission?" I asked Notch.

"Yes you did. Congratulations, by the way. I liked how you handed things down there." He said.

"Thank you for the tips; you've been of great help. I thought I would be completely alone for these missions."

"This is also another important lesson for you." Notch said. "No matter how big the problem is, we can always count on someone else to help us. Don't think you're alone to face your issues."

"Alright."

"For your next mission, I have something new for you. This one is quite interesting, and it will test some of your communication and your teamwork skills." Notch said.

"Interesting. Any other hints?"

"No. You'll have to see and discover for yourself. As usual, remember to call me if needed. Also, you only have two more patch notes available. If you really want to use one of them for whatever reason, you just have to let me know."

"Hmm, can I use one of the patch notes to remove my inability to craft things?"

"No. Everything that has been included in the Herobrine update and its following patch notes cannot be removed."

"Okay, got it. I'll keep that in mind."

"Keep up with the good job, you're doing great. Good luck and good bye." Notch said.

I blacked out.

Day 21

I woke up in a new server. Notch didn't tell me anything about my new mission, but he seemed really interested with this one. I wonder what I'll have to face next... And to my surprise, I was again really close to the house of a player.

I did the same thing when I was in Parker's server: I hid in the woods and observed the house to know more about the player I was about to help. That way, I could learn more of their story and how I could help.

I saw one player coming out of the house and heading to a nearby river. He was fishing in the river when another player, a girl, came after him.

"What are you doing now, Patrick?" She said.

"I'm fishing, Susan." He said. "You know, getting some food!"

"I know you're fishing! Didn't I tell you to get ready to fight the Endermen? Why did you decide to go fishing right now?"

"Because, uh… I'm sick of eating carrots and apples all day, I suppose."

"Gosh, I told you and Joe to get ready and you just keep playing around. I don't know why I must have such silly younger brothers like you two!"

"But Susan, we also need

food, don't we? What's the reason for going after the Dragon if we can't eat?"

"Sigh… I'm done with you two. I'll go craft my swords. And if you find

Joe, tell him to return home because we need to get ready." Susan said.

"Okay, alright. Gee, why do you have to act as our mother?"

"Because I am the oldest sibling and because you two are irresponsible." Susan said.

"That's not fair… No one gave you the right to do that!" Patrick said.

"Don't be silly, Patrick. Just tell Joe to come home. I'll get to work."

"Alright. I will."

Susan returned to the house and Patrick went to the woods to search for his brother. So according to my observations, there are three players living in one house, and they are siblings.

Also, they want to hunt Endermen and to fight against the Dragon. But wait a moment, what am I supposed to do here? I have never beaten the Dragon myself! How can I help people with something I have never done before?!

Day 22

I watched the three siblings all day, trying to find the perfect opportunity to get in touch with them. Later, I saw Patrick coming out of the house again, and he was alone. This was my best chance to talk to him.

I walked towards him and tried to talk.

"Hey Patrick! Can I speak with you for a moment?" I said.

"Uh... Wait. Why do you have white eyes? Don't tell me you

are... Herobrine?"

"Yes, I am Herobrine." I replied, unable to lie due to my patch notes. "But I am here to help you…"

I barely finished my phrase when Patrick grabbed a sword and ran to me.

"Herobrine! I will defeat you! Get out of here!" He yelled.

"No, you've got it wrong! I am not bad! I just want to help…"

"Susan! Joe! Get out here! Herobrine wants to attack me!"

Joe came out of the house and when he saw me, he did the same thing. He grabbed a sword and attacked me. I was now running away from two players, swords in hands, evading their attacks while trying to explain everything.

"Please stop! I want to help you!" I said.

"Stop lying, Herobrine! We know everything you've done to others! You are a prankster!" Joe said.

I ran towards the house, and saw Susan opening the door.

"I'm screwed. She will attack me too!" I thought.

"What are you two doing now?" Susan said. "Stop!"

"But Susan… This guy is Herobrine!" Joe said.

"Yes, I am Herobrine, but I am here to help you! I don't want to hurt anyone." I said.

"Lies! You want to play a trick on us, don't you?" Patrick said.

"Patrick, Joe, enough! Let's hear him out!" Susan said. "So, are you really Herobrine? What are you doing here?"

"Yes, I am Herobrine, and

despite my fame as a griefer, I am actually here to help you with whatever you need. I know everyone dislikes Herobrine because it's a creature known for destroying worlds and all,

191

but I can promise you I am not here to do that."

"Well… I don't know if you're really Herobrine or not, but you don't look threatening to me. Let's go inside and you can tell us your story." Susan said.

"But Susan…" Joe said.

"Enough, you two! Susan said.

Day 23

At the human's house, I told the humans everything about my past and my story and why I was there to help them.

"And that's it. I've been Herobrine for almost a month and my duty is to help other players." I said.

"This is a long story. I don't know if I believe everything you just told us, but I guess you're being honest." Susan said.

"So, can you really speak with animals? Awesome! Could you tell the fishes to come out of the river so I can catch them easily?" Patrick said.

"Patrick, we've got more important things to deal with!" Susan said.

"She's right, Patrick. The Endermen, remember?" Joe said.

"Oh right, the Endermen." Patrick said.

"From what I heard, you guys want to hunt the Endermen and go to The End, correct?" I said.

"Yeah, we need to defeat the Dragon." Susan said.

"But why?" I asked her.

"Our parents created this server a long time ago. They raised us here, and they worked hard every day to give us a good life. They've never been able to defeat the Dragon themselves, and now they're too old to do that anymore. The Dragon gets stronger every year he remains alive, and he must be extremely powerful right now. We want to defeat him to honor our parents." She said.

"Beautiful story. Now I know why Notch sent me here." I said.

"So, you're gonna help us with Dragon?" Patrick said.

"Yeah, I suppose. I mean, I have never defeated the Dragon myself… I don't know why Notch sent me here, but if I am in this world then I should help you guys with that."

"Sure, why not!" Susan said. "Welcome aboard, Herobrine."

"Thanks. I'll do my best." I said.

Day 24

Now that I've been accepted into their group, I need to find out what the three siblings need to do next.

"Our next plan is to hunt the Endermen." Susan said. "But those monsters are tough to fight, and don't appear often."

"Well, I saw one the other night but he teleported away..." Patrick said.

"We need to find a way to get them before they teleport." Susan said.

"I think I know how." I said. "I am neutral to hostile mobs and the like."

"Really?" Susan said.

"Yes, that's one of my perks as Herobrine. I could get behind them and attack before they notice."

"That could work. Do you need a sword?"

"Yes please, I can't craft anything myself."

"That's too bad. Crafting makes things easier."

"Yeah, I loved to craft when I was a regular player. I really hope to return to normal and craft items again once I finish my quests." I said.

Susan gave me a Gold Sword and we went after the Endermen.

Day 25

In our first day hunting the Endermen, we searched inside large caves and tunnels. During the day, that's where you can easily find the Endermen and hunt them. But we didn't find a single one, and we waited until it was night to search again.

During the night, the same problem: no signs of Endermen in the area.

"Where are all of them?" Susan said. "I don't know why it's been so difficult finding them."

"I have never hunted Endermen before, but I know they're hard to get by." I said. "Perhaps we shouldn't stay in one location."

"You're right, let's search inside the house for the Endermen." Patrick said.

"Patrick, I really hope you're being sarcastic." Susan said.

"Yeah, Patrick! Endermen inside our house? Don't be silly! It's easier to look for 'em inside the river, for instance."

"Gosh... I must be adopted." Susan said.

We looked for the Endermen in the area and didn't find them. And it was too late, because the sun was coming out.

Day 26

We rested during the day to search for the Endermen during the night. And now, we walked north to look for the creatures. And fortunately, we found them. Lots of them in a single region.

"Woah! Look at that! We've got a ton of Endermen here!" Patrick said.

"This is it. I'll go get them. You three, stay here and make sure the other monsters don't attack you." I said.

"Okay, good luck Herobrine!" Susan said.

I grabbed the Golden Sword and I did the same with the monsters in

Parker's server – I simply attacked the Endermen one by one and defeated them, grabbing the Ender pearls in the process.

"Wow, he can attack the Endermen without dragging their attention! How is that even possible?!" Patrick said.

"I guess he really is Herobrine, like he said." Susan said.

" But… If he is Herobrine, then he will destroy our house?!" Patrick said.

"Don't be silly, Patrick. No, he won't. If he wanted to destroy our house, he'd have done it already." Susan said. "We need to trust him; he really wants to help us."

I defeated over 30 Endermen in the course of 10 minutes. It was easier than I thought. I grabbed all the Ender Pearls and returned to the group.

"Here you go; I suppose this is enough, isn't it?" I said.

"Yes. We only need a few to throw and find the portal, and the others will be used to turn on the portal to The End. Thanks a ton for the help, Herobrine! I never thought I would use this phrase in a context like this." Susan said.

"Haha, you're welcome! I'm glad to help. Now, let's go back home because there's still work to do." I said.

"You're right, Herobrine! We need to go fishing!" Patrick said.

"Patrick, just no. Please." Susan said.

Day 27

Back at their house, they gathered all items and resources to fight against the Dragon into a single chest. Ores, Armors, Weapons, Tools… They had everything, except one item.

"Now we just need one thing to complete the mission." Susan said.

"And what is it?" I said.

"Fishes!" Patrick said.

"Of course not, silly." Joe said. "We need to make the portal."

"Well, Joe is not absolutely wrong." Susan said. "But we need Blaze Powder, in order to activate the Ender Pearls and open the portal."

"Blaze Powder, that item that only drops from the Blazes in the Nether?" I said.

"Exactly. It's a very hard item to obtain and Blaze Powder is required to create the Ender Eyes."

"I see. Well, we can use the same tactic again! I attack the monsters and you just back me up." I said.

"Great. We'll build the portal to the Nether tomorrow, now we need to find some Obsidian." Susan said.

We went after the Obsidian needed to craft the portal to the Nether.

Day 28

Down at the mines, Joe and Patrick mined all day to find Obsidian in the deep caves underground.

"Y'know, we could easily make some Obsidian by placing water and lava together, but we don't have any buckets to take lava." Susan said. "And my only Diamond Pickaxe is about to break."

"Obsidian is not that hard to find, though." I said.

"Speaking of …., look at that." Susan pointed to the left of the cave where we were, and we found some Obsidian under a water source.

"Alright, I'll mine this out. Be careful guys, there might be lava under the ground here." Susan said.

"Okay sis! We're good!" Patrick said.

"I'll help you take the Obsidian blocks." Joe said.

Susan mined the Obsidian using her Diamond pickaxe, and Joe picked up the blocks. She removed 12 Obsidian blocks, more than enough to craft one portal.

"Alright, we're good to go. Time to return home. But where's Patrick?" Susan said.

"Well, he was here with us." I said. "Where did he go?"

"Patrick! Where are you?" Joe said.

"Patrick! It's time to go home! C'mon!" Susan said.

And Patrick was nowhere to be seen.

"Patrick is always giving me a headache…

Gee." Susan said.

We searched for Patrick inside the cave and we finally found him next to one of the underground tunnels. He was staring at a dark cave.

"My gosh, Patrick! Why did you leave the group? It's dangerous to be alone here, you know that!" Susan said.

"I know sis, I just wanted to take a look around." He said. "I found a cool box! Can I take it home?"

"A box?" Joe said. "What type of box?"

Patrick pointed to the box inside the dark cave.

"That one with a little Zombie spinning inside!" He said.

It was a Zombie spawner.

"Run guys! It's a spawner!" I said.

Susan grabbed Patrick's hand and we all ran out of the cave. Despite not attracting any monsters, I would not be able to protect the three players from a Zombie attack like that. Once inside the cave, Susan taught Patrick a lesson.

"Never, ever again leave us like that! Did you hear me, Patrick?"

"Okay sis, you don't have to be mad!" Patrick said.

"Mad? I am furious! We could've been attacked by those Zombies! Herobrine can't save all of us at the same time!"

"Okay, I promise I will never leave you guys again." Patrick said.

We returned home safe and sound.

Day 29

Now that we had the Obsidian, Susan crafted the portal.

"There we go. The portal is ready. Now Joe, have you got the flint and steel?"

"Yes."

"Alright, go on and activate the portal."

Joe used the flint & steel and the portal was activated.

"Nice! Alright guys, let's grab our stuff from the chest and we're ready to depart for the Nether." Susan said.

We came back home and dressed up with the armors. Everyone got a sword and a few tools to use. Ready to enter the Nether, we returned to the portal and crossed to the other side.

"This is it guys, we're in the Nether now. Remember to be extremely careful, as the place is"

Before Susan could finish her sentence, a massive explosion tear the portal apart. It was a fire ball shot by a Ghast.

"Run, everyone! Hide in that cave!" I said.

We rushed to the cave under a rain of fireballs. We made it to the cave safely, but the portal had been destroyed by the Ghast.

"Phew… We're safe." Joe said.

"Yeah, we just need to be careful with the Ghasts here." I said.

"Very well. We need to rebuild the portal first because once our mission is over we'll come back running at it. Joe, have you got the remaining Obsidian blocks and the flint & steel?"

"Uh... No. Have you?" Joe said.

"Joe... You gotta be kidding me, right?

You're the one who activated the portal!" Susan said. "Where's the flint and steel and the blocks?"

"Yeah I did activate it, but you're the one who built it, Susan! The Obsidian blocks should be in your inventory!"

"I can't believe this... I think I left the Obsidian blocks in the chest when we got the other items..." Susan said.

"And I did the same with the flint and steel..." Joe said.

"Okay, so what does that mean?" Patrick said.

"It means... we're stuck in the Nether." I said.

Day 30

Our mission to enter the Nether and take the Blaze Powder for the Ender Eyes was just beginning. However, we've got a bigger problem in our hands right now.

Susan forgot to bring the Obsidian blocks to the Nether with her, and Joe left the flint & steel in the chest as well. The portal has been destroyed by a Ghast, and we're stuck in this dangerous place with nothing but our armors and weapons.

How are we supposed to come out? I may not be attack by any creatures since I am Herobrine, but the three of them are normal players. For how long can I protect them? We need to find a way out, and fast!

The mission to find the Blaze Powder can wait; our priority right now is to get back to the Overworld safe and sound.

Book 3: Redemption

Day 1

After becoming Herobrine, I have been teleported to several different worlds, tasked to help other players in dire need. My latest mission was to assist the siblings Susan, Joe and Patrick in their mission.

Our first task as a group was to hunt the Endermen and grab the Ender Pearls. Relatively easy, considering my skills to hunt monsters without being attacked by them. We accomplished the mission

together in just a single day.

But our second mission was to enter into the Nether and hunt the Blazes. We needed the Blaze Powder to craft the Ender Eyes, and we created the portal to get the items. But now, the unexpected happened: a Ghast shot down our portal and we are now trapped in the Nether!

Susan forgot to bring the Obsidian blocks with her, and Patrick left the flint and steel inside the chest. We can't even restore the portal, nor activate it once again. In other words, we are in big trouble and it's gonna be tough to find a way out of here.

Day 2

Inside the Nether, we did everything we could to stay away from the Ghasts. We spent the day inside a cave, planning our way out.

"We're so dead. We're dead. Dead." Joe said.

"Joe, shut up! I need to concentrate." Susan said.

"Don't worry Joe, we're not gonna die." Patrick said.

"Maybe if we could find two Obsidian blocks somehow…" Susan said.

"I think the Pigmen drop Steel, and we may find some Flint mining the Gravel here in the Nether." I said.

"Good idea, Herobrine!" Susan said. "Let's go get the flint and steel needed to activate the portal."

"But we can't leave this cave. There are some Ghasts flying above us right now!" Patrick said.

"Those Ghasts are gonna be the real problem here…" Susan said.

"I can go there and get the flint and steel we need, but I don't know about the Obsidian." I said.

"Yeah I'm also out of ideas." Susan said. "Even with the flint and steel, we can't activate the portal without the two Obsidian blocks needed to complete it. The Ghast destroyed those blocks."

"I'll try to come up with something…" I said.

And then, I remembered I had one trick up my sleeve.

Day 3

Today, I invoked Notch to ask for help.

"Notch, can you please come here?" I said.

"Sure, why not." Notch said. "The Nether, huh? Nice to see you're here."

"Notch, we're stuck in here! How do we get out?" I asked him.

"Stuck? Where's the portal?"

"We built the portal, but the Ghast destroyed it. The other players left the Obsidian blocks and the flint and steel in their chest." I said.

"Ah, that happens quite often. That's why players should always keep those items in their inventories. It's an important lesson for new players and alike."

"I know... But can you give me any skills to take us out of here?" I said.

"Maybe, but that will use one of your patch notes." Notch said. "You have two left."

"Alright, I will use one of them." I said.

"Let me see... I can teleport you to the normal world if you want." Notch said.

"That'd be great! Thank you! But can the other players see you?" I said.

"No, only you." Notch said.

"You just have to tell them I teleported you all to the world above."

"Okay. Let me go get them." I said.

I gathered everyone where Notch was, and I told them what was going to happen.

"Are you sure, Herobrine? Notch is here with us and he'll teleport us back to the Overworld?" Susan said.

"Yes! I can ask for his help when needed,

but I got only two requests left. I will use one of them to teleport us out of here."

"Alright, I believe you. After all, you defeated all those monsters without being attacked. Let's go then, we are ready!" Susan said.

"Okay Notch, do your thing!" I said.

Notch teleported everyone to the overworld. Surprised to be back, the players cheerfully celebrated their return.

"We did it! We are back!" Patrick said.

"That's outstanding. Thank you Herobrine, and thank you Notch, wherever you are!" Susan said.

"Thanks, Notch. I really appreciate it."

"You're welcome, Herobrine." Notch said. "You only have one request left now. And be more careful the next time you go to the Nether."

"Sure, we will!" I said.

Notch vanished and we all returned to the house.

Day 4

Back home, we prepared ourselves once again for the trip to the Nether.

"This is it, guys. We've been given one chance to make things right. Let's take everything we need for the trip so we won't get stuck in the Nether again." Susan said.

"Okay, I won't forget the flint and steel now." Patrick said.

"Can I take the Obsidian blocks with me now?" Joe said.

"Sure, Joe. I'll personally give them to you, though." Susan said. "We can't make the same mistake again. By the way, what's a rookie mistake... It's hard to believe we fell for that."

"Yeah... And we've been playing here for so long." Patrick said.

"Don't worry guys, it happens!" I said. "I myself have never been to The End, or even tried to get there. I think we all become better humans when we make mistakes and learn from them."

"Nice one, Herobrine!" Susan said. "Beautiful words."

"Thank you. I learned that from Notch." I said.

"Very well. Let's get ready for the trip! We won't fall for the same trick twice." Susan said.

I'm glad to see they're excited to go to the Nether. It's good to keep the hopes up when we have a mission ahead of us.

Day 5

Now that we're all set to go, we headed to the portal and crossed it. A new portal was created inside the Nether, right next to the one destroyed by the Ghasts.

"Here we are!" Susan said. "Quick, run to the cave!"

We all rushed to the same cave where we hid before. From there, we made a new plan to find the Blaze Spawners.

"The Blaze Spawners are always inside a Fortress." Susan said. "According to my researches, the Fortress is generated inside the Nether in random locations, so we should choose a direction and just go for it until we find one."

"A Fortress? Do they have a castle with a king too?" Joe said.

"No, Joe. It's a Fortress with monsters!" Patrick said.

"Once we find the Fortress, we need to infiltrate it and search for the Spawner. Beware, though: Blazes are dangerous monsters who deal a massive amount of damage when attacking with their fire balls."

"Gee. I'm really scared now!" Patrick said.

"Don't be. Together, we can defeat them." I said.

"We have Herobrine by our side, brothers! Fear not, our victory is certain!" Susan said.

We left the cave and walked east from the portal.

Day 6

Now that we were walking inside the
Nether, we watched out for Ghasts and
other potentially lethal monsters.
Fortunately, my Herobrine ability
allowed me to avoid even the Nether
monsters, and I served as the bait for
the creatures.

"No signs of a Fortress so far."
Patrick said.

"What is a Fortress?" Joe said.

"A Fortress is like a huge purple
wall, Joe. If you see any of those, let us
know." Susan said.

"Oh, a purple wall? Like that
one?" Joe said, pointing to the North.

228

"Gosh, that's a Fortress far in the distance! Well done, Joe! You have a very good sight." Susan said.

"Ah thanks, I can see things from far away." Joe said.

"Good job. Let's go everybody; we need to investigate the Fortress and search for the Blaze spawner!" Susan said.

The Fortress was really far from where we were, but we had no doubts it was one. Finding a Fortress was not too much of a big deal, but reaching this one certainly was not the easiest part of our duty.

"Guys, watch out! There are some Ghasts flying ahead!" I said.

We hid in a small corner and waited for the Ghasts to go away.

"Phew. Why are there so many Ghasts in this world? I've been to the Nether before, and I don't remember seeing so many of them!" Susan said.

"Mom and Dad used to say that the longer the Ender Dragon remained alive, monsters would spawn more often in the worlds."

Patrick said.

"Oh, I remember that too." Joe said.

"Maybe that's why..." Susan said. "Anyway, this is a real challenge on its own. Evading all Ghast attacks and sneaking inside the Nether. Never thought it would be this hard."

"I'll tell you what, guys. I'll go ahead and see if there are any other monsters in the area. If everything's clear, I'll send you a hand signal and you follow me." I said.

"Deal! Go on, Herobrine.

Lead the way!" Susan said.

I went ahead and cleared the way for the rest of the group. I saw some

Zombie Pigmen, but these wouldn't attack the players. The Ghasts roamed the area and eventually left. It took us long, but we made it to the Fortress. Now, it was time to search inside the Fortress and find the Blaze Spawner.

Day 7

Inside the Fortress, we had to be extra careful. Finding the Blaze Spawner would not be as easy as finding the place.

"So, the Blaze Spawner should look like the normal Spawners we have in the Overworld, right?" Patrick said.

"As far as I know, they look alike. The only difference is the creature inside the cage should be a Blaze." Susan said. "Any thoughts, Herobrine?"

"Honestly, no." I said. "I myself have never hunted the Blazes, nor gone to The End."

"Really?" Susan said.

"Yes. In fact, I've never advanced this far into the game." I said.

"Nice, so now you'll be able to do so with some friends!" Patrick said.

"Yeah, I suppose. I'll do my best to help." I said.

We searched inside the Fortress throughout the corridors and the different rooms. We didn't find anything, and we even ran into some Wither Skeletons which were easily defeated by the group.

"Good job everyone, let's keep fighting together and we'll make it to the end!" Susan said.

As we searched even further

into the Fortress, we found a single chest inside a dark corridor.

"Wow, a chest!" Joe yelled.

"No Joe, don't open it! It could be a trap!" Susan said.

Regardless of her warning, Joe opened the chest and grabbed the items inside.

"Look! Gold and Diamond. We are rich!" Joe said.

"Two Diamonds and a Gold? Why would they keep ores inside the Nether?" Susan said.

When we looked back, we saw 10 Wither Skeletons coming in our direction.

"Run everyone!" I said.

I tried to slow down the Wither Skeletons as much as I could while the others ran out of the Fortress. They made it in safely and I

went after them.

"Phew. That was close." Susan said. "I told you not to open that chest, Joe!"

"But we are rich now, sis!" Joe said.

"We can't get rich with that much ore, Joe." Patrick said. "We can barely craft a tool with that."

"Well, at least I can use those Diamonds to craft a sword." Susan said.

We didn't find the Blaze Spawner, but it was time to call it a day. Things were getting dangerous inside the Nether, and we had to regroup and prepare a new plan.

Day 8

Inside the Fortress, we needed to find a way to get to the Blaze Spawner as fast as possible.

"We are running low on provisions…" Susan said. "We can't stay for much longer in here."

"You're right." I said. "I'll try to find the Spawner by myself. You guys can take the upper floors and we'll meet up here again in one hour to inform the others if we've found the Spawner or not."

"Good idea, Herobrine. Come

on guys, we need to find the Spawner fast, or we'll have to return to the Overworld empty handed." Susan said.

"Good luck, guys! See you all in one hour." I said.

"Good luck!" They said.

We all left the room and everyone searched their floors. I looked everywhere but the Spawner was nowhere to be seen. Is there a Fortress without any Blaze Spawner? I was about to give up when I found one right next to a lava pool.

"Yes! Now I just have to call the others and…"

But then, I realized it would be much better if I simply dealt with the Blazes by myself, instead of putting the group in danger. After all, I do not attract monsters unlike the normal players. I grabbed my sword and went after the Blazes.

"Come here now, Blazes! I'll make this nice and quick." I said.

I attacked one Blaze with my sword, but it didn't despawn. Instead, the creature looked at me and shot a fireball!

"Wow! What are you doing?!" I said.

The other Blazes reacted as well, and all creatures shot me with fireballs. I had to run away quickly before they got to me.

Back at the room, I waited for the others.

"Guys, I found a Blaze Spawner!" I said.

"Really? Good job! We only found two other chests…" Susan said.

"But there's more to it… I attacked a Blaze and they all counter attacked!" I said.

"What? How's that possible? But you are Herobrine!" I said.

"I know, right. They shouldn't attack me… I don't know what

happened." I said. "Maybe they are different from the Overworld monsters with regards to that?"

"Well, the Zombie Pigmen do not attack players. But when you attack one, all other Pigmen in the area will defend their friend." Susan said.

"That's another thing I didn't know." I said.

"This collective behavior may be the reason why the Blazes attacked you. Therefore, we must be extra careful if we're dealing with monsters that are ready to attack in group."

"Exactly. But if we work together, we can do it!" I said.

"Alright, let's go to this Blaze Spawner and see what we can get from it." Patrick said.

Day 9

I took the group to the Blaze Spawner. Aware of the Blaze's hostility, we stayed a few feet from the Spawner in order to watch the spawn behavior of all Blazes.

"Okay, bear in mind the Blazes will attack altogether if one of them gets hurt." Susan said.

"Exactly. We need to take them out at the same time, rather than fight it one at a time." I said.

"How are we gonna do that?" Patrick said.

"First, we need to know how many of them are out there." I said.

"Next, we need to know how often a new Blaze spawn."

"I see. And if we know their spawn rate, we can defeat all Blazes at the same time without getting attacked from behind." Susan said.

"Exactly! Plus, it's good to know if other Blazes will spawn because we need a lot of Blaze Rod."

"Great plan, Herobrine. You're really clever!" Susan said.

"Thanks! Alright, let's keep them on watch now."

We waited all day and we counted at least 17 different Blazes flying over the Spawner. Seventeen! That's a lot of Blazes in a single area.

"Gee… My plan seemed perfect, but they're in a greater number than I expected!" I said.

"You're right… We can't go in there and fight them." Susan said.

"Why not? I can beat them up!" Joe said.

"No Joe, you can't. No one can do that. They'll outnumber our group." Patrick said.

"Well, what should we do? Any other plans?" I asked them.

"Do Blazes sleep?" Susan said.

"I don't know. Do they?" Patrick said.

"That's what I'm asking." Susan said. "If they sleep, we can get them while they're unaware."

"We can wait and see for ourselves." I said. "But we're running low on supplies, we either get this done today or we'll have to come back some other day."

"You're right. Let's wait and hope we get lucky with this plan." Susan said.

And we waited for the Blazes to sleep... without actually knowing if they do.

Day 10

Later that night, everyone in the group was asleep. I woke up and I realized we had a job to do.

"Guys, come on! We feel asleep. Wake up; we need to take the Blaze Rods!" I said.

The rest of the group woke up and we came back to our duty.

"What happened? Have we missed them?" Susan said.

"No, they're still there, floating around…" I said.

"So Blazes do not sleep… Now we know that." Patrick said.

"Wait a moment..." Susan said. "Look at their eyes."

We looked at the Blazes and they all had their eyes closed. In fact, they were floating asleep.

"They are sleeping! That's how they sleep!" Susan whispered to us.

"Shss, keep quiet guys. This is our chance to take them down." I said.

We quietly approached the Blazes and we attacked together one of them. The Blaze was defeated during his sleep. The others did not wake up.

"That's it! Let's repeat what we've done!" Susan said.

We attacked the other Blazes, one by one. We collected all Blaze Rods and in a short period of time, we had over 17 Blaze Rods available.

"Nicely done, guys! Now maybe just a few more and we can go home..." Susan said.

Behind her, 10 Blazes spawned from the Spawner and flew over us.

"Get out of here!" I said.

We ran away from the Spawner as the Blazes shot fire balls. We barely escaped their attack intact, but we made it.

"Gosh, why is it so dangerous in the Nether?" Patrick said.

"Because this land does not belong to the Overworld, Patrick." Susan said.

"Well… We've got some Blaze Rods. I think this is enough for what we need." I said.

"Agreed. We'll put these Rods to good use. Besides, we cannot stay much longer in here. Come on guys, let's head back home." Susan said.

"Already? But it was getting so much fun here!" Joe said.

"Joe, it's not funny when you're being attacked by a bunch of Blazes." Patrick said.

"Yes, let's find a safe cave to stay and then we can go back to the Overworld."

We slept in the Nether for the last time before going home.

Day 11

In the morning, we left the cave and went to the Nether Portal.

"Alright, good bye Nether! It was nice visiting you." Susan said.

"Come on, let's go back." I said.

Everyone crossed the Portal and we were back in the Overworld.

"Home, sweet home!" Patrick said.

"Feels good to be back." Susan said. "Congratulations, we are

one step closer to our final goal!"

"We have the resources, now comes the last and most difficult part." I said.

"Don't worry. Together, we can beat that Ender Dragon." Susan said.

"I hope you are right. I have never seen the Dragon. I don't know what to expect!"

"Just relax. I have never seen the Dragon neither, but our parents always told us to remain calm. The Dragon is strong... but with the right team, he's easily defeated. Our parents never had a good team to fight along them. Just the two of them couldn't beat a Dragon that big. But now that we are a team of four, we can destroy the Ender Dragon and restore this world to normal!"

"Alright, if you believe so then I shall follow you." I said.

"Okay, let's get rid of the Dragon!" Joe said.

"Calm down, Joe. We need to find the portal first."

"Portal? Again?" Joe said.

"No Joe. It's a new one, the End Portal." Susan said. "I'll craft the Ender Eyes needed to find the Portal. We'll stock up on food and other items and leave soon."

Day 12

Now with the Ender Eyes required to find and activate the End Portal, we just had to find the place and put the Pearls inside. Oh, and defeat the Dragon, of course. I forgot to mention that part...

"Okay, we've got the armor and the weapons needed to fight the monster. The potions are here and we have the Ender Eyes. Let's leave our house and find this thing once and for all." Susan said.

"What potions do you guys have?" I said.

"All types of potions. Patrick has been preparing them for years, just for this day. We have strength potions, healing potions… For all needs and uses." Susan said.

"Can I use an Invisibility potion?" Joe said.

"No, Joe. We only have two of those because they're hard to prepare. We will use the potions when needed."

"And what is this one for?" Joe said, grabbing a potion from Patrick's backpack.

"Hey! Give it back, Joe!" Patrick said.

Joe ran from Patrick, who chased his brother.

"Gee… I don't even know why they're my siblings. Just, how?!" Susan said.

Joe ran in circles with the

potion and he accidentally dropped it on the ground.

"Oh no! See what you just did? You wasted one of our Invisibility potions, Joe!" Patrick yelled.

"Can you stop messing around, please? We need to focus here. If you continue playing like that, you won't fight the Dragon with us."

"No! I won't do this anymore, I promise. I want to defeat the Dragon!"

"Then stop fighting against your brother. You're the youngest here, remember?" Susan said.

"I hate to be the youngest… Why can't I be the oldest?"

"Because you were born last, silly." Susan said. "Off we go, then. We've lost one of our potions thanks to Joe, but I suppose one Invisibility potion will do."

"Sure, let's go." I said.

Day 13

Now we're on a journey to find the famous End Portal. The Portal which I've never seen myself with my own eyes, only heard of.

"I'm really excited to find this Portal. I've never been there to the End." I said.

"We'll do that together then. No one here has seen the Portal." Susan said.

"I saw a Portal!" Joe said. "I win!"

"No, Joe. That's the Nether Portal, it doesn't count." Patrick said.

"Yes, it does!" Joe said.

"No, it doesn't!" Patrick said.

"Yes, it does!" Joe said.

"Enough, you two!" Susan said. "Gee, can't we have a single peaceful day with you two around?"

"Sorry sis, but he started it." Joe said.

"No, you did!" Patrick said.

"Alright, I don't care who started it. Now let's focus on the quest we have here, okay?"

"Okay sis! I am helping!" Joe said.

Susan threw the Ender Eyes and we followed their lead. She picked them up and threw again. The Ender Eyes lasted for over 20 throws, before breaking up and disappearing. We had over 20 spare Ender Eyes to throw, so we had 400 throws to find the Portal before running out on resources. The other 14 we had should be saved to activate the End Portal.

Day 14

Searching for the End Portal was not easy at all. We had to take turns in throwing the Ender Eyes, and even so it didn't seem to make much progress.

"Gosh... I'm so tired of throwing these pearls into the air..." Patrick said.

"Keep going, Patrick." Susan said. "We are really close. I can feel it."

"Close? We've been doing this for two days! Plus, we only have 4 Ender Eyes to throw; the rest would be to activate the portal! What if we run out of them before finding the Portal?" Patrick said.

"We can build a monument where we stopped and return home. Once we have more Ender Eyes, we come back to the monument and continue our progress." I said.

"That's the plan." Susan said. "One step at a time, brother. That's how you achieve your goals."

"I am so tired of walking... I can't stand this anymore." Joe said.

"Come on Joe, weren't you the one who was anxious to defeat the Dragon? Keep up!" Susan said.

"But this is so boring... I just want to fight... I don't want to walk..." Joe said.

"I'll tell you what, Joe. If you keep up, you'll be the first one to receive the potions to fight against the Dragon. I'll give you a strength potion and a healing one." Susan said.

"Really? Do you promise?" Joe asked her.

"Yes, I promise. Now let's go! Don't stop!"

"Okay, I won't stop! I want to drink the potions to defeat the Dragon!" Joe said.

Susan motivated Joe to keep looking for the End Portal. We all were exhausted and wanted to take a break, but our main goal was more important. We needed to find the End Portal and get to the dragon!

Day 15

We continued searching for the Portal with the Ender Eyes. It was my turn to throw the Ender Eyes and follow them. We were running out of Ender Eyes and we didn't know how far the Portal was...

"I suppose we'll have to wait a few more days before actually finding the portal, Susan." I said.

"I tried to be positive about it, but I guess you're right. We will break all Ender Eyes before actually finding the End Portal." Susan said.

"But can't we just find it today?" Joe said.

"It's not that easy, Joe." Patrick said. "Only the Ender Eyes can show us where the Portal is. We can't find it without the pearls."

"Exactly. Mining the world and randomly searching for the Portal on our own is completely out of question." Susan said.

"Well. I just broke another Ender Eye." I said. "Only one more."

"Okay. Let's use it until it goes out and then we'll mark the spot. We can resume the search when we have more Ender Eyes to use in our search."

I threw the Ender Eyes to the air and it immediately went left.

"Left? Why did it turn left so quickly?" Susan said.

"I don't know. Maybe we're very close to the Portal, otherwise the Ender Eye would not take turns like that." I said.

"You're right! Keep throwing it,

Herobrine!" Susan said.

I picked it up and threw again. The Ender Eye guided us ahead. We all knew it was very close,

I threw the Ender Eye and we followed it. The Ender Eye just pointed ahead and we continued. I picked it up and threw again, but this time the Ender Eye did not float. It remained on the ground.

"What happened? Why isn't it floating?" Susan said.

"No clue. Let me try again."

I picked it up and threw it in midair, only to see the Ender Eyes returning to the ground and resting

on the surface.

"Wait a moment. This is it! This is the place where the Portal is located!" I said.

"Wow, that's true! The Ender Eye is resting above it!" Susan said.

"Portal! Portal!" Joe said.

We picked our shovels and started digging the area. The Portal was right underneath and we were steps away from it.

We dug down all the way to the rockbottom and we found an old cave.

"This cave must be the place where the Portal is. Watch out for traps or monsters." Susan said.

We explored the cave and we found some doors and even old switches leading to empty corridors and rooms. It was like an underground fortress, and somewhere inside that place the Portal would be found.

"Let me try the Ender Eye just once more." I said, throwing the Ender Eye in the air. The Ender Eye turned right and stopped by a wall.

"There we go. The End Portal must be behind this wall! Take it down, guys." I said.

Everyone got their pickaxes and we removed

the stone wall. On the other side, we saw a big room with the End Portal in the middle.

"Wow, we found it! Nice job, guys!" Susan said.

"Yeah! Portal! Portal!" Joe said. "I wanna fight the Dragon! I really do!" Joe said.

"You must be really excited to fight this dragon, huh." Patrick said. "Let's see if you'll remain this happy

when you actually see the creature."

"I will! I love dragons!" Joe said.

"You what? But you're not supposed to love the Ender Dragon, Joe! We need to defeat it!" Patrick said.

"I know. I will defeat it! You don't have to worry because it will be easy!" Joe said.

"If you say so…"

Susan placed all Ender Eyes in the End Portal, and it activated. The pitchblack frame appeared in the middle.

"Amazing... So this is the path to The End!" I said.

"Yes. Looks like a starry night." Susan said. "It's beautiful to look at."

"Can I jump in already?" Joe said.

"No, Joe! We need to rest a bit! Come back here." Susan said. "We'll enter The End tomorrow. Now sit quiet and relax."

"We need to get ready before fighting the Dragon." Patrick said.

"Any plans, Herobrine?" Susan said.

"Oh, not really." I said. "Like all of you, this is my first time in The End. I am completely clueless about everything. I don't even know what to expect!"

"Haha, I get you. Don't worry; I'm sure we'll all make it through together." Susan said.

"Sure. Let's do our best, guys!" I said.

I was really nervous to go to The End, but also happy to share this experience with such great friends like Susan, Joe and Patrick. My duty as the Herobrine has been more like a life experience than a punishment for my sins. I thank Notch for giving me this opportunity!

Day 16

Today was the big day. The day we would face the evil Ender Dragon and, if defeated, I would conclude my mission in this server, which was to help these three siblings overcome the Ender Dragon. But this was more than just my duty: it was also my personal challenge to defeat the Dragon for the first time.

We woke up in the morning and prepared breakfast before jumping into The End.

"Good morning, everyone." I said.

"Morning. I just woke up too." Susan said.

"What a night! I could barely sleep." I said.

"Same here... I didn't sleep at all. I guess I'm too anxious to go in there and get over with this once and for all." Susan said.

"Same with me. I'm tired now." Patrick said. "What about you, Joe?"

Joe didn't answer.

"Joe? Wake up, Joe. It's time to go defeat the Dragon." Patrick said. "Wait a minute... Sis, Joe is not here!"

"What? Where did he go, then?" Susan said. "No. Oh, he couldn't have done that..."

"Is he inside The End already?!" I said.

"Gosh, Joe! And I told him to always wait for us!" Susan said.

"Quick, we need to get there! Breakfast will have to wait!" I said.

"Sure, grab your weapons and all the potions. We're getting inside now!" Susan said.

We packed up and jumped into the Portal together. On the other side, we spawned over yellow blocks in a dark world.

"The End sure is… scary." I said.

"It is. Come on, we need to find Joe before the Dragon is alerted." Susan said.

We left the spawn and entered a big floating island, full of Endermen everywhere.

"Don't look at their faces… Be careful." Susan said.

"I'll try to find Joe for you guys, since I don't startle the creatures." I said.

I searched everywhere but Joe was not there. I left Susan and Patrick behind and went even further into that place.

"Come on, Joe. Where are you? Your sister and your brother are worried with you." I thought to myself.

A few feet ahead, I saw Joe staring at the sky.

"Joe!" I yelled. "Joe! What are you doing there?" I ran to meet him. "We've been really worried with you! Why did you enter The End without waiting for us?"

"Because I wanted to see the Dragon first! I was really excited to come here." Joe said.

"I know you like Dragons and wants to fight it, but come with us! We need to find the Dragon and fight together!"

"But the Dragon is already here, I am fighting it!" Joe said.

I looked up and I saw the Ender Dragon coming straight at us.

"Get down, Joe!" We both laid on the ground and the Ender Dragon hovered over us.

"Run! We need to meet up with the others!" I said.

We returned to where Susan and Patrick were, and grabbed our swords.

"Joe, thank heavens you're safe! What did I tell you about running away from us?" Susan said.

"I just wanted to see the Dragon, sis. I didn't run away or anything!" Joe said.

"Guys, the Dragon is coming! Let's defeat him first and we can talk later!" I said.

"Fine. I'll continue this later, Joe." Susan said. "Here guys, take the Strength potions and drink it up."

Susan distributed the Strength potions and we drank it immediately.

The Dragon was coming again and we had to hit him this time.

"Here he comes! Raise your swords and hit him when he gets close!" I said.

The Ender Dragon flew right next to us and we hit him with our swords. The monsters screamed and continued flying.

"Nice hit! Keep up, we've got this!" Susan said.

The Dragon turned around and came back.

"I guess this Ender Dragon won't give up. Let's do the same thing!" I said. We raised our swords and waited for him.

But this time, the Ender Dragon pulled a trick on us. Before getting closer, he opened his mouth and spit a fire ball at us.

"Watch out!" Susan said.

The fire ball passed by us and didn't hit anyone.

"Gee, this Ender Dragon is not playing around! We need to be more careful from now on." I said.

The Ender Dragon flew high and approached a few pillars in the area. The pillars had some sort of jewel on the top.

"What are those pillars for?" I said.

"I don't know…" Susan said.

The jewels shot laser beans at

the Dragon, and it restored the life he had lost.

"What?! Those rocks restore his life?!" I said.

"Oh no! Quick, where's your bow and arrow Patrick? Try to destroy those rocks!" Susan said.

"I got this." Patrick said. He grabbed his bow and shot the first jewel, which exploded upon the impact.

"Amazing! Good one, Patrick!" I said.

"Patrick is a very skilled archer." Susan said.

Patrick got the other pillars and, one by one, he destroyed them. The Dragon tried to stop him and spit fire balls at him, which he successfully evaded.

"Alright, now shoot the Dragon and he will be forced to

come right at us!" Susan said.

Patrick shot some arrows at the Dragon. Angry, he turned around and flew straight at us at full speed.

"Gosh, he's coming up too fast!" Susan said.

"We won't be able to hit him properly. Just

raise your swords and try to hit him as much as you can!" I said.

The Ender Dragon passed by us at full speed but we managed to hit him. Injured and without being able to heal, the Ender Dragon was even angrier and striked again. But this time, he landed next to us and tried to hit using his tail.

"Careful! Get away from him!" I said.

We ran and the Dragon came after us on his paws. He was really fast despite being big, and we tried to escape his claws. He hit Susan with his tail, and she fell on the ground.

"Susan! Are you alright?" Patrick said.

"Sure, but he got me! Don't let him hit you, guys!" Susan said.

The Dragon approached Susan and I attacked him with my sword. I hit him as many times as I could and he spit fire balls at me. Luckily,

I am Herobrine and I can stand a few shots. I am more resistant than normal players.

"Agh… I'm getting really tired… I won't be able to take him down…" I said, backing up.

"Careful! The Dragon is about to spit a fire ball again!!" Susan said.

The Dragon opened his mouth and aimed at us. Suddenly, someone strikes him from behind and the Dragon screams – it's Joe.

"Joe! What are you doing?" Susan said.

"I am fighting the Dragon! I love to do this!" Joe said.

I grabbed the Invisibility potion and gave it to Susan.

"Here Susan, drink it up. You need to recover now, so stay away from danger." I said.

"But then I'll leave you all to the Dragon by yourselves!" Susan said.

"Susan, you should trust your brothers." I said. "Joe and Patrick may not be the smartest brothers in the world, but they sure are skilled fighters and will do their best to protect their sister. Let them handle this and you'll be surprised with the outcome." I said.

"Okay, Herobrine. You are right, I should rely on them more."

Susan drank the potion and the three of us attacked the Dragon. Joe hit him with his sword, and Patrick used his bow and arrow. I tried to get the Dragon with my sword.

We hit him several times and the Dragon flew up high, severely injured. He wouldn't survive much longer. He flew over our heads and shot fire balls again. He was really weak and had to land on the ground once more. That's when Joe got into action again.

"It's your chance, Joe! Do your best!" I said, tired of fighting and watching him from the distance.

Joe sliced the Dragon and hit him with his sword. He was very fast and the Dragon didn't resist the attacks, despawning after a few minutes.

"We won?" Joe said.

"Yes Joe, we won!" I said.

"Victory!   Congratulations, guys!" Susan said.

Now that the battle was over, we just had to collect the Dragon Egg and all of the experience points.

Day 17

Back in the Overworld, we take a look at our battle spoils.

"So much experience... I can easily enchant my bow now!" Patrick said.

"I can level up my sword with these points." Susan said.

"I can craft a brand new fishing rod now!" Joe said.

"Good to see you all have new plans for your future." I said.

"And you, Herobrine? What have you got in mind now?" Susan said.

"Well, my future is not mine to be decided, at least not in my Herobrine form. Now that I have completed my mission, chances are I'll be teleported to Notch's world tomorrow, leaving you guys behind."

"Really? But can't you stay a little longer?" Patrick said.

"Unfortunately I can't. I've fulfilled my duty here, and we've beaten the Ender Dragon. Now, I believe I will be assigned to help a new server in need. Anyway, I just want to say that I've had a lot of fun here. I totally forgot I was Herobrine for the most part of my time, and thoroughly enjoyed it as if I was playing with you too."

"It was really nice of you Herobrine. We wouldn't have done it without your support and help!"

Susan said.

"Thank you, and I must say thanks to you three for giving me the opportunity to defeat the Ender Dragon. As a player myself, I am very proud of my achievement. Before I get teleported, I'd like to say thanks once again, and if possible, I'll try to return here to visit

you guys some other day."

"Please do. We'll be waiting for you!" Susan said.

Day 18

I woke up in the white room again. I was in Notch's world, as it usually happens after completing a mission.

"Oh, I'm here." I said. "I'm partially glad to be here, but also sad."

"And why's that?" Notch asked me.

"I'm glad because it means I've successfully completed my mission, correct?" I said.

"That's right."

"But I am also sad because I really liked to play with those guys. They were really friendly and nice."

"Good to know that you've not only played along with your friends to reach your goal, but you've bonded with them. You've created new relationships and discovered the true meaning of friendship. This is the most important aspect of a multiplayer world like this one."

"True. When I was a troll, I didn't mind ruining the fun for others. Now, I'd rather have fun with them instead, which is a lot better. This journey has opened my eyes in many ways."

"Good. That's what I intend to do, after all." Notch said. "You're here to learn how to play properly, not only to pay for your mistakes. And I'm really proud of what you've turned out to be."

"Thanks, I'm actually happy to be Herobrine." I said.

"I am sure you are. Soon enough, I'll assign you a new task. But now you need to rest, because you have just defeated the Ender Dragon." Notch said.

Day 19

Notch didn't say much about my next assignment until the next day.

"Anyway, here we are." Notch said. "Ready for your last mission?"

"Last? So this will be my last time as the Herobrine?" I asked him.

"Exactly. You've completed all missions so far with great results. I'm happy to see you've always been a kind and generous person all along, who just needed some guidance to get out from the trolling path."

"Hehe, I guess that's a way to put it." I said.

"Now, you've done all kinds of things in these two months as Herobrine. You've helped Ned learn how to properly treat his horse, you saved Parker and his friends from the tyrant Richard and you also lent Susan, Patrick and Joe a hand in defeating the Ender Dragon. You've done all types of tasks, from easy to very hard. And for your last mission, I'll give you something relatively easy."

"Relatively easy? What do you mean?" I asked him.

"This mission may sound harsh at first, but it will be really easy when you find out what's behind it." Notch said. "Now go. Good luck in your last assignment."

And I blacked out.

Day 20

I woke up in another server once more. Well, at least this is my last time in a mission. Once this ends, I'll be able to return to my normal life! I totally forgot to ask Notch if he could send me to the sibling's server once everything's over, but I'll see about that later.

Right now, I've got a mission to complete. I don't know what it is about, who I must help, or what I need to do. The sooner I find the people in need, the better.

Now, if only I had spawned

next to the city or house or whoever I am supposed to help... Notch spawned me in the middle of nowhere again! I am lost which direction should I take? Well, I'll just pick one and go like I did for my other missions.

If I spawned here, then I mustn't be too far from my objective.

Day 21

Walking around inside this server is bringing me many memories. I have the feeling I've been here before, but I don't remember exactly when. What is this place? I feel like I know where I am supposed to be...

Am I in one of my friend's servers again? Maybe the people I have already helped before now need my help once again? I didn't understand exactly what was going on, but the more I walked ahead, the more familiar things were.

I stopped by a beach and I saw

a jungle biome in the distance. Immediately, my past just flashed inside my head; my entire life since the day I started playing on my very first server, and I realized where I really was. This was the server where I was kicked out for stealing!

I went to the jungle to see if the village was still there. And to my surprise, the place was intact. The people inhabiting the village were working as usual, and I saw all the houses I had destroyed had been completely rebuilt.

What does Notch want me to do here? The last time I was here, I was trolling and griefing these players for kicking me out without any solid evidence of my crime. Now, I am back here and I'm tasked to help them. And how will I do that?

Day 22

I needed to find Joseph in that village. I'd approach and talk to him in private to see what I could do for them. I can't walk right into the village and say "Hello, I am Herobrine and I am here to help."

Especially after what I did to them. These players are scared to death of the name Herobrine because of my actions. Now I understand why Notch sent me here: for my final mission, I am supposed to help the people I hurt the most, and also clean Herobrine's image that I ruined

myself.

I have been watching the village all day, trying to get a grip of what's going on these days. I saw Joseph at one point, going from one house to the other, talking with other players and doing daily chores.

I can't approach him like that because he'd call the others and chaos would ensue. Just think about it, the terrible Herobrine who supposedly has been playing pranks and trolling the players for a whole month, finally shows up and offers his help.

What would they think? Of course they wouldn't react so well. I can't take any risks... I need to go to Joseph's house in the morning before he goes out, so I can talk to him in private.

Day 23

I waited all night for the players to go to sleep. In the morning, I sneaked into Joseph's house and entered when no one was watching. Joseph was having breakfast and he was surprised to see me.

"Wait... You're Herobrine?" Joseph said.

"Yes, I am Herobrine. I'm glad to see you recognized me." I said. "But fear not, my friend. I am not here to do any harm."

"What do you want?"

"I want to talk to you. I am well aware of what this village has been through, and how the other players are scared of my presence. But I am here to prove that Herobrine did NOT do that to your village."

"Wait… So you really are Herobrine, and you want to prove you didn't troll us? What's the point?" Joseph said.

"Herobrine has been known for griefing and trolling players and servers alike for several years. Unfortunately, this is because bad players have taken advantage of his name to troll for the sake of having fun. This is unfair for Herobrine's reputation, and I want to clean it up."

"I see. So, who did it?" Joseph said. "Who trolled us?"

"Mark." I said.

"Mark? Wait… That guy we kicked out of here? Gosh… I should've known that."

"As Herobrine, I am sworn to only tell you the truth, and the truth only. I can't lie or deceive, as per my creator's request." I said.

"And who's your creator?"

"Notch, the developer." I said.

"Notch?"THE Notch? The guy who created the game?!" Joseph said.

"Yes. He created me to help players in need."

"Wait, that's just too much for me to believe."

"No worries. I can prove I am Herobrine because I am different from normal players. I can talk to animals and I am not attacked by the monsters."

"Okay, if you can prove me that you really are Herobrine, then I'll trust you." Joseph said.

"Sure thing. I'll be outside the village at midnight, waiting for the monsters. You can go there and bring the other players with you if you wanna see it for yourself."

"Okay. We'll meet you there."

Day 24

It was past midnight when the players came out of the village. They stayed within the village's main gate, still skeptical about my presence.

"Hey there, everyone. I'm glad you are here. This will be a quick test to prove that I am Herobrine. I do not intend to hurt anyone, nor destroy or grief your city. I know what you've been through in the past, but I am here to make things right. Now, pay attention. See those Zombies over there? I'm gonna punch them and they won't chase

me." I said.

I went to the Zombies and punched them several times. The creatures just stared at me and did nothing in return. The crowd was impressed.

"See? This kind of thing is impossible to do even with potions. As Herobrine, I can easily travel around this world and help people in need. That is my objective here, and I am willing to assist you in everything I can."

"Okay, you might be Herobrine, but how can we be so sure that you really want to help us?" Joseph said.

"Believe me Joseph, if I wanted to destroy your city, I'd have done that a long time ago. Give me a chance and tell me what your needs are, you won't regret it." I said.

"Fine. I'll give you a chance,

Herobrine. We need your help with a little something, but I am not sure if you can help us with that." Joseph said.

"I'll be glad to try."

"Come by my house tomorrow in the morning so we can talk." Joseph said.

Day 25

In the morning, I stopped by Joseph's.

"Good morning, Joseph. May I come in?" I said.

"Morning. Sure." He said.

I entered the house and sat by the table.

"So, what do you need help with?" I said.

"Well, here's the thing. We've been having trouble getting food."

"How so?" I said.

"The crops don't grow in this village. In fact, every time we plant seeds, they disappear." Joseph said.

"Disappear?"

"Yes. They disappear over the night. A few months ago, there was this guy who worked as a farmer for us. He joined the village and planted Wheat to help the other players. But his Wheat disappeared twice in a row, and we suspected that he could be stealing it from us."

"I see. And then?"

"We kicked him out. I mean, it was the village's decision but we should've put more thought into it... The guy's name is Mark, and it is now clear that he was not stealing anything. I guess I understand why he trolled the village for so long..."

"And the crops keep disappearing?"

"Yes. We've tried everything. We tried planting seeds in an indoor

301

farm, underground, on the top of the trees in artificial farms, but nothing works. Not even our melons are growing anymore. We live with what we catch every day, such as fish and the apples we pick from trees but it's hard not having a food supply."

"I understand your issue. I'll look into it and see what I can find." I said.

Day 26

So the village has been having the same problem for three months. The crops are not growing properly, and the players don't know what to do anymore. It was not my fault after all, at least I'm glad to know I am not the one who did something wrong.

But now, I've got a big problem on my hands. What's causing this? Why can't they plant anything? Who, or what is taking out all crops and seeds? I need to investigate and go further into this

matter.

I spent the day looking around, asking people some questions and verifying the farms. The players are still wary of my presence, but they've been of great help. I couldn't identify precisely the cause of the problem, but certainly it is not being caused by a person.

According to the players, the seeds and even the crops disappear sometimes. It disappeared right in front of their eyes. One day, a group of players planted a Wheat crop and stayed up all night on watch. They saw the seeds popping out of the ground and disappearing.

Some say the village is cursed, while others believe the biome is decaying. Either way, I need to find an answer, and I might have a trick up my sleeve for that.

Day 27

In the morning, I invoked Notch to help me with my last mission.

"Notch, I need some help. Again." I said.

"Go on." Notch said, spawning behind me.

"Notch. I understand what I am supposed to do here. Fortunately, I've gained the player's trust. Partially, at least. Now, I'm in a dead end here. I'm supposed to find the culprit responsible for getting rid of all seeds and crops. What should I do? Can

you lend me a hand?" I said.

"Very well. You still have one wish, remember?" Notch said.

"Yes, I do."

"Would you like to use your last wish to solve their problem?" Notch said.

"Yes."

"Okay. Let me check my database." Notch said.

"I don't know if you can find the exact reason why the seeds don't grow properly here…" I said.

"Done. I've found it." Notch said.

"What?! That was fast!" I said.

"Of course, I've got data of everything in this world. Anyway, the seeds are not growing here anymore because of a biome shift."

"Biome… shift?" I said.

"Yes. As the game updates, the biomes receive new tweaks and upgrades. With time, some biomes may suffer drastic changes to their climate and area. In this case, this jungle biome has a desert biome climate."

"So, they can't grow seeds because it's supposed to be a desert? What about the trees that are here?"

"Everything that was part of the biome before the changes remain intact. But planting new trees and seeds now may prove inefficient because of this change. Therefore, I will use your last wish to return this biome to normal." Notch said.

"Can you do that for me?" I said.

"Sure. Give me a day. Tomorrow, tell the players that everything will be back to normal and they can plant new crops again."

"Thank you so much, Notch! I really appreciate it!"

And Notch disappeared.

Day 28

Today, I told the players of what Notch did to the biome.

"Wait, so you just talked to Notch and solved the issue? I don't believe it." One player said.

"It's true, guys. The biome has been restored to normal. You can plant your crops again and they'll grow just fine." I said.

"If that's the case, thank you Herobrine. You really helped us like you promised." Joseph said. "If only we hadn't kicked that player out of

here for this…"

"Don't worry. That player deserved it because he trolled the village and pulled pranks on you." I said.

"How do you know that?" Joseph said.

"Because I am that player. I am Mark." I said.

When I finished my sentence, by body began to shine. I had a strange feeling inside me, and suddenly I was back to normal... I was Mark again.

"Wait... I've gone back to normal! I am me again! Yes!" I said.

The other players around me couldn't believe it. Herobrine was Mark!

"Wait... What just happened here? Mark, is that you?" Joseph said.

"Yes, Joseph. Hey everyone, I'm Mark. The guy who you kicked out, and the guilty guy who griefed you. I've been serving Notch as Herobrine for almost two months to pay for my crimes. It seems I've completed all my duties, at last." I said.

"Mark... You were Herobrine the whole

time?" Joseph said.

"Yes. I've been sent to other servers to help players in need, and my final mission was to come here and settle things down. I also need to apologize for my actions and for being so childish. Instead of finding an alternative, I wanted to get my revenge on you. I am deeply sorry and I will understand if you don't forgive me for what I did."

"Mark, I forgive you. And I believe most other players here forgive you, too. We removed you from here without any proof, without any evidence that you stole the Wheat. We also have our share of guilt."

"But what I did was even worse. Trolling is never acceptable, no matter the circumstances. Anyway, I'm back to my normal life. I'd love to help you guys with anything else you may need now, though I no longer have my Herobrine powers with me."

"Sure, Mark. Welcome back to the village!" Joseph said.

Day 29

Today, I helped Joseph and the others with the crops. Everyone cheered and celebrated when we planted the first seeds and they actually remained planted, without disappearing or popping out.

Now the jungle biome was back to normal and the players could plant their crops safely without worrying about getting food elsewhere. Having a stable food supply is one of the most important aspects of life in this world, and now

the jungle village is safe.

I've restored my own position in the village, and also cleaned Herobrine's reputation. I promise to never, ever take advantage of the name of others.

Day 30

I woke up in the white room again.

"What? Why am I here?" I said.

"I just wanted to congratulate you for your efforts." Notch said, sitting by his desk.

"Hey Notch. Thanks for taking me back to normal." I said.

"No problem, you deserved it." He said. "I'm really happy to see how you've grown up during these

months as Herobrine."

"I must say, it was all thanks to you. I owe all of that personal growth to you. What would I be if I continue trolling and griefing others? I'd be banned from all servers I joined, never truly enjoying the fun of playing this game the way it's meant to be as a player, with friends and others."

"Exactly. Griefers never take this in consideration when they're destroying and wreaking havoc on other servers."

"You could have solved everything on your own, correct? I mean, you could have restored that biome even if I wasn't there."

"Exactly. But if I did so without your intervention, the players would think Herobrine was the one behind everything for the rest of their lives. And you've fixed that for me."

"I appreciate the opportunity. I had a lot of fun being Herobrine. Oh by the way, I know I am not in a position to ask anything, but…"

"Go ahead. You're my most successful Herobrine so far, I can grant you a personal wish if that's what you want."

"You know, I've made so many friends during my journey… Ned, Parker, the three siblings… But they've never met the true me, only Herobrine. I'd love to stop by their servers and say hi. I don't know if I'm asking too much, but…"

"Here you go." Notch handed me a book. "These are the IP Addresses of the three other servers where you've been before. Feel free to visit them whenever you want."

"Really? Amazing! Thanks a lot Notch, you're the best!"

"I'm pleased to help. Anyway, congratulations again and have fun in your new journey. I am sure there are still a lot to discover out there, and a lot to do."

"As for Herobrine, what will be of him?" I said.

"Other players will take on his role, just like you did. So if you ever see another Herobrine roaming around, don't be afraid. They might be looking after others."

"Alright. Good bye! See you around!" I said.

Day 31

Back at the jungle village, I grabbed my booklet and went through all IP Addresses. Now, I could easily go back and visit Ned and his horse, Parker and his city, and the siblings Susan, Patrick and Joe.

I'm excited to go back and talk with them as Mark, and see what they've been doing now that most of them have overcome their problems. Not only that, but I also intend to go on new adventures with them, and

have fun with everyone.

I've truly discovered what this game is all about. Griefing and trolling only ruin the whole experience for everyone, including the griefer himself. I know what I must do from now on, and how to live my life.

And if I ever see a Herobrine knocking by my door and offering a helping hand, I'll be very glad to let him in and accept his offer. Herobrine may be an infamous hoax, but I'm sure we'll be able to change this with time!

Book 4: The Herobrine Program

Day 1

Wow! I haven't touched this diary in such a long time. Time flies, indeed. The last time I wrote anything here was when I was transformed back into my human form, after serving Notch as Herobrine for two months.

Just reading back all my stories from my time as Herobrine brought me nostalgia. Ah, that was so much fun! Frightening at some point, but is still fun and rewarding experience.

After becoming human again, I started living with Joseph and the other villagers in the Jungle Village. I have been working the crops, planting wheat as well as melon, carrots, potatoes and even sugarcane. My crops are the most beautiful around!

Not only that, but life has been very peaceful ever since I returned here. I haven't heard of Notch again, and I have taken the time to visit my friends from the other servers. I still visit them occasionally, just to see the three siblings Patrick, Joe and Susan fighting over the most menial things, or to see if Ned is taking good care of his horse. Or even to check on Parker, the new leader of his server, who has been fair and just to everyone living with him.

As for Notch, last time I heard, he retired from game development. He wanted to rest after working so hard on this amazing game. I can't blame him; it must be tough looking after so many things every day. I hope I can still meet him again one day, though.

Day 2

I never saw another Herobrine in this world. Not once I came across a Herobrine helping other people. I guess I was the last Herobrine to assist people... Or maybe the other Herobrines who were eventually hired by Notch went somewhere else.

Honestly, I kind of miss being Herobrine. It was always so unpredictable, never knowing where you would end up in the next morning, or who you had to help. I was always getting into some weird situations, but it was an interesting way of living.

Not that I am complaining about my current life. I really, really enjoy this place. It's just that it gets boring sometimes... I don't know. I can't complain, but I do at the same time. Go figure!

Day 3

I was working the fields as usual when Joseph stopped by, like he does every week.

"Hey Mark!" He said.

"What's up, Joseph?" I replied.

"Working much?"

"Yeah, I am sorting the seeds and preparing the soil for the Potatoes. Nothing interesting, you see." And I chuckled.

"Well, crops are always interesting. They feed our people, so that is definitely worthy of my attention!" Joseph said. "Anyway, tomorrow is Carl's birthday and we are throwing him a surprise party. Want to come over? There will be cakes and plenty of food! You don't need to bring anything. Just a gift for him, if you want."

"Sure, sounds fun! I will see what I can get him as gift." I said.

"Great. 6PM at his house, we'll be there before he returns home." Joseph said.

"Alright, thanks for the invite." I said.

Joseph left, and I was wondering what I could get for Carl. Perhaps a basket of assorted vegetables and grains? Nah, I had already given that to him last year. But I suppose food is a great gift for

all occasions, isn't it?

Day 4

Despite having plans for a surprise birthday party for a friend, my day was about to change completely.

I woke up in a white room. I knew that place... It was the place where Notch used to work! But... How? Why? Didn't Notch retire or something? Or maybe that was just a rumor...

Then that's when I saw him – a redheaded guy, frantically typing on a keyboard and staring at a white PC screen. He didn't seem to be bothered by my presence, and I approached him from the back while he was sitting at his white leather chair.

"Uh… Excuse me? Is this Notch's room? Who are you?" I asked the man. But as he turned around, I recognized him.

"Hello. I am Jeb." He said.

"JJJEB! Yes!" I repeated. "You're Jeb! The developer! Right?"

"Exactly. Nice to meet you, Mark."

"Nice to meet you too, sir! Oh, wow. How lucky am I? Not only did I meet the creator and one of the main developers of the game, Notch, now I get to meet another lead developer! I think not many people have this opportunity!"

"You're right, not many people do." Jeb said. "And you're only here because of your history."

"My… history?" I said.

"Yes. Your history, your record, whatever. The point is, Notch always talked a lot about you as Herobrine, Mark."

"He... did? That's awesome." I was honored to be mentioned in such high regard by Notch himself.

"Yeah. He liked the way you used your powers to help others. You know, the Herobrine Program has been active for over 6 years and you were probably the best Herobrine we had. At that time I was working on the other game features, but I read all reports written by Notch."

"That's great." I said.

"Indeed. We have had around 60 or 70 Herobrines. I can't remember. Even after Notch left the team to pursue other endeavors, the Herobrine Program continued – and I have been in charge of implementing it for the next generations of Herobrines."

"Cool! So the name is Herobrine Program... Well, makes sense."

"I invited you – or better yet, teleported you here today because I need to ask you for a favor, Mark." Jeb said.

"Wait... Let me guess. You want me to be Herobrine once more?" I was so excited to become Herobrine again, I couldn't keep it to myself!

"No." Jeb replied, much to my dismay.

"WWhat... Wait, why not?" I asked, saddened by the response.

"I don't want you to be Herobrine because you have already done your share. We need to hire other people to be Herobrines – mostly, griefers and pranksters who must pay for their wrongdoings. You see, we have six active Herobrines in the world right now..."

"Wow, six? That's cool!" I said.

329

"...And they're all failing their objectives." Jeb said.

"Huh, that's... Bad." I said.

"Yep. Sadly, the previous 10 Herobrines have also underperformed. Their results were not good. Some of them even had to be kicked out because, instead of helping people, they used their powers to grief even more. The ones who actually did try to help others, were unable to do so." Jeb said.

"Sorry to hear that..." I said.

"Like I said, right now we have 6 active Herobrines who need your help, Mark." Jeb said, pointing

at me.

"Me? Where do I come in?" I asked.

"I want you to provide assistance to my Herobrines." Jeb said.

"What?! But, but... Herobrines are supposed to assist others! How can I assist someone who is assisting others? Even saying that was weird!" I said.

"Like I mentioned before, you were our best Herobrine. You have fulfilled all of your duties with ease. I could sit here all day and grant all those Herobrines as many wishes as they want, but I am not their Genie in the Lamp. I can't waste my time helping them, because as you know, I am also a lead developer. I have got other matters to attend to. What better person to take the role of Herobrine's assistant than the best Herobrine himself?" Jeb had a good point.

"That's... Impressive, Jeb. Really impressive. But I don't know if I can take the role..." I said. "It has been such a long time, I don't know if..."

"Ah, come on. You've been dying to be Herobrine again. I saw it in your diary, or journal, or whatever." Jeb said.

"You read my diary?!" I was scared.

"Of course. You are living in my world, buddy. Nothing escapes from my eyes. Now tell me, Mark – do you want to have an exciting life once again? Please, I just need your help with these 6 Herobrines right now. Once you have finished helping them, you can go back to the Jungle Village. If you refuse, you can also go back and there will be no hard feelings on my part. It's just that... I can't ask anyone to do this." Jeb asked me.

"Sigh... I can't refuse, Jeb. Even though I am not sure if I am capable of helping them, this sounds like a great opportunity. I won't lie, I enjoyed being Herobrine; however, I don't know what exactly a Herobrine assistant is."

"You'll have the same powers as Herobrine, plus one more extra skill: you will be able to grant one of their wishes." Jeb said. "Only one. I know Notch offered you three, but we have reduced to one because people have been abusing these wishes."

"Awesome, I can do that!" I said.

"Great. Now, go tell your Villager friend about your new adventure. I will teleport you here later to provide all info on your quest. Farewell!" Jeb disappeared, and I was back at my house in a puff of smoke.

Day 5

I went back to the Village and I
stopped by Joseph's house to talk to
him. I managed to get there just before
he left for work.

"Hey Joseph." I said.

"Oh, hello there! We missed
you at the party, man!" Joseph said.

"I know, I totally bailed on that.
I am very sorry… I wanted to go but I
had an… appointment with someone."
I said.

"Really? Someone from the
Village?" Joseph asked.

"Listen, Joseph. I have got something to tell you. Since you are my closest friend here in the Village, I will only tell you, so you can pass the info along."

"Sure, you can tell me anything. What is it?" He asked.

"Remember that time when I was Herobrine?"

"Sure, I do remember. You helped us and you also helped other people from other servers, right?" Joseph said.

"Exactly. Turns out, the developers need my help once more. This time, however, I will have to help the other Herobrines who are having trouble fulfilling their objectives."

"Really?! That's so cool!" Joseph said. "So you'll be like, a Coach Herobrine?"

"Huh… Well, an assistant of sorts but I actually liked that. Coach

Herobrine…. It has a nice ring to it, doesn't it?"

"Yep, ha ha ha!" Joseph laughed. "Okay Mark, that sounds so cool. Obviously, we are going to miss you because you're the best farmer we've got. But don't worry, I know this is also very important and if the developers called for your help, then it must be urgent. I will send Clara and Josh to take care of the farming while you are gone. Sounds good?"

"That's fantastic, Joseph. Thank you so much." I said. "Sorry for leaving in such short notice, but it was also a big surprise to me."

"Nah, don't mention it. You did a great thing back then – you completely shifted the biome of our Jungle, man!" Joseph said.

"Actually, it was Notch who did it on my request… But thank you nonetheless! Yeah, it feels really good to help. I guess that's why they want me to lend a hand to the other Herobrines."

"Sure thing. Oh and if by any chance one of those Herobrines stop by our Village, please come with them!" Joseph said.

"I will see! I don't even know where they are right now, but I will go talk to Jeb soon." I said.

"Jeb?! Woah, the game developer! You're so lucky when it comes to meeting celebrities... I envy that!" Joseph said. "Anyway, go for it Mark. We'll be waiting for you and for your next stories as Coach Herobrine! Go get 'em!"

"Thanks Joseph! I will definitely come back, and I will tell you guys everything about my new journey!"

This feels awesome. I can't wait to go out there and travel, see new servers and meet new people!

Day 6

I was teleported to the white room again, as Jeb said.

"Ready for your assignments?" Jeb asked me from his white chair.

"Sure am!" I replied. "Can't wait to become a Coach Herobrine!"

"Coach Herobrine? That sounds nice." Jeb said.

"It does, right? My friend Joseph gave me the idea for the name." I said.

"Great. Before I dispatch you out there, I will give you an overview of all six Herobrines, their personalities, who they are as humans, and their new missions. You can choose which one you want to help first, okay?" Jeb said.

"Cool! Go on, I am listening." I said.

"Here we go." Jeb said. "They are as follow:

1st Herobrine: Manu.

She's a girl who has griefed her friend's server, when her friend refused to let Manu become an admin.

Personality: Manu is a calm and peaceful person, but don't let it fool you. She can be decisive when she wants.

She has been working as a Herobrine for five days.

Failed her two previous assignments. Her current (and 3rd) mission is to help two friends get along over a disagreement.

2nd Herobrine: Koala

It's not his name; it's his nickname

because he really likes Pandas and Bamboo. Don't ask me why they nicknamed him "Koala", though. Became Herobrine not because he was a griefer, but because he must overcome his fears in order to be a better player.

Personality: Has fear of dark and heights. Friendly but also a coward.

Herobrine for four days.

Failed one previous job and completed one.

It's his last mission. Must guide a lost traveler through a dark cave, because the traveler wants to find his lost dog.

3rd Herobrine: Parson

Didn't grief, but he deceived some Villagers and stole their items after conducting illegal trades with them.

Personality: Thinks he's the smartest man alive. Can be stubborn at times. Has a good heart, though.

Herobrine for a week.

Failed three jobs. If he fails one more, he will be banned.

Next mission: A small village was surrounded by Illagers. He must find a way to rescue them. It's one of the two hardest missions of all six Herobrines for a simple reason: Illagers are hostile towards Herobrines unlike other Aggressive Mobs.

4th Herobrine: Lara

Lara lived in a village with other friends. One day, they entered The Nether to get some items. They were attacked by Ghasts and instead of helping her friends who were in danger, Lara ran away because she was too scared. The Ghasts destroyed the Nether Portal as soon as Lara returned to the Overworld, alone, leaving her friends behind.

Herobrine for five days.

She is not a bad person; however she needs to learn the value of being loyal to friends and others.

Failed two jobs. Last job before being banned.

Next mission: Enter the Nether and rescue her stranded friends.

5th Herobrine: Klei

One of the most successful griefers in the world. Klei ran amok destroying villages as he pleased. The reason it took us so long to find him is that Klei was also a good hacker. He managed to hide his IP for a long time. We tracked him down and now he must pay for all his crimes.

Personality: Always charming and friendly, Klei can talk people into doing whatever he wants. This is probably the hardest Herobrine for you, because he will be quite the challenge.

Herobrine for three days.

Failed two missions. The reason is because he doesn't know how to help others.

Next and last mission for him: This is probably the hardest mission of all six. Klei must find a way to make a Peace Treaty between three enemy kingdoms in one of the most populated servers of the game. There are over 100.000 people involved between all three Kingdoms.

6th Herobrine: Wanessa

Kind woman who has done a lot to help others. Wanessa wanted to become a Herobrine because her Village was being attacked by Endermen. She still hasn't figure out why her Village in particular is targeted by them, who are nonhostile creatures by default.

Personality: Kind and nice to everyone. Wanessa's goal is different from the others, since she personally requested me to become Herobrine in order to help others. As such she will not be banned in case she fails her mission, but failing it would mean the Village will be attacked by Endermen forever.

Herobrine for ten days.

Mission: Find a way to help the Village and discover what's behind the Endermen attacks.

So as you can see Mark, we have some very easy missions and also some extremely hard missions. You can take whichever one you prefer." Jeb said.

"Wow, I really liked the description of these. Can I have a copy?" I asked.

"Sure, I will provide you with patch notes for all missions within your own journal." Jeb said.

"Awesome! Anyway, I guess I will start with the easier missions because I haven't done this Herobrine thing in a long time, you know?"

"I completely understand, Mark. You can choose any mission. I will let the other Herobrines know that help is on their way, and that they must continue their job in any way they can until you reach them." Jeb said.

"Alright. In that case, I will go in order. Send me to Manu, please." I said.

"Manu it is. Good bye and good luck. Remember, only one wish per Herobrine and it cannot be anything too game changing or impossible." Jeb said. "If the wish cannot be completed by any reason, you will be notified by an alert."

"Okay! Thank you Jeb." I said.

"No, thank you, Mark." Jeb said, snapping his fingers.

I blacked out.

Day 7

I woke up in a Dark Oak forest. It was noon, because the sun was high up in the middle of the sky. I got up and looked around – there was nothing but trees.

"Well, time to complete my first quest." I said.

I walked around searching for any clues and then I found two houses. Yes, two wooden, nice looking houses in the middle of nowhere, some 30 meters apart from one another.

"Well that's strange… This isn't even a human village; it's just a couple of houses in this forsaken land!" I thought.

That's when I saw it – or even better, her. My Herobrine! Manu was sitting by a tree, watching over the houses and writing something in a book.

"Hello there." I said, right behind her.

"You scared me!" She said. "Are you… Are you the…"

"Coach Herobrine? Yes I am. The name's Mark." I said. "How are you doing?"

"Well you look just like a normal player…" Manu said.

"Yeah, my looks remain the same but I was sent by Jeb to help you. I guess he refrained from changing my appearance to Herobrine because it would be weird seeing two Herobrines walking around, huh. By the way, I didn't know there was a female version of Herobrine! Your hair looks great."

"Thank you." She said. "This is actually my real hair. In fact, even my clothes are all the same and my appearance too. The only difference is that my eyes turned white and my clothes changed colors – blue pants, teal shirt…"

"Yeah, the Herobrine colors. I get it. Quite interesting." I said.

"Yep… Anyway, can you help me?" She asked. "I haven't done so good in my previous missions… I need to complete this one, or else…"

"Absolutely. What's the deal?" I asked her.

"The players will come out soon. Let's go back to the forest, where we can talk in private." She

said.

Day 8

Manu explained to me her new mission today.

"According to the description from Jeb, you must help two friends get along over a disagreement. Is that correct?" I asked.

"Well, yes it is." She said. "These two guys were friends but they had a fight over a diamond pickaxe. They used to share the pickaxe because it's enchanted and pretty rare. It has the Fortune IV enchantment."

"Wow, that's probably the best enchantment for pickaxes." I said.

"Exactly. Now they are arguing over who's the owner of the pickaxe and haven't come to an agreement. It's a petty dispute, I know, but somehow I need to figure this out. Otherwise…"

"Don't say anything, Manu. I understand." I said. "You see, the secret about helping people is not trying to change the way they think. Like, you cannot get inside their heads and force them to change their minds. This has to come naturally. You need to show them the path to redeem themselves with one another."

"Wow… That was really deep." Manu said.

"Uh, I guess it was… I didn't even think it through." I said.

"No, you are right! Please, continue." Manu said.

"Anyway, have you already talked to them?"

"No. The reason I failed two of my previous missions was because the players were scared of me and didn't want to accept my help." Manu said. "I am afraid of scaring these two and not completing my quest."

"I see. I also had this problem very often back when I was Herobrine." I said. "I even had to run away from two brothers with swords in their hands, running after me! Luckily their levelheaded sister was there to save me. But in this case, I will see what I can do."

"Thanks, Mark." Manu said.

Day 9

We spent the day watching the two players to understand their routine before acting.

"I watched them for a day before you arrived. They have some habits; the guy with the house on the left side likes to go fishing every now and then. The guy with the house on the right side rarely leaves the house; I guess he spends most of the day inside the mine under the house."

"I see. In that case, it's better if we talk to the guy on the left when he's out fishing." I said. "Despite being enemies, one might be startled by the other in case one screams upon seeing you."

"Good call. Then what?" Manu said.

"Then you just have to wind it!" I said.

"Wind it?! I mean, isn't there some sort of script that you used to follow, or…"

"No, you have to be yourself! Just think of a way to help them resolve this. You can do it, Manu!"

"Okay…I can do it…" Manu said, not so confidently.

We waited all day to see if the player will leave his house to go fishing.

Day 10

After a whole day and night, the player finally left the house with his fishing rod. Manu was asleep by the bushes and I woke her up when I saw him leaving the house.

"Manu, wake up! The guy's on the move, let's go!" I said.

We both tiptoed our way behind him, always following the player from afar. Minutes later he stopped at a lake and threw the fishing line into the lake. I asked Manu to stay behind a tree while I introduced myself to him.

"Just follow my lead, okay? When I give you the sign, you come out!" I said.

"Wait, what sign?" She was confused.

"You'll see!" I said, leaving her behind the tree.

"Oh, hello there!" I said out loud to the man.

"Huh, hello." He seemed mildly startled but greeted me normally. "Pardon, I didn't know there was someone else out here."

"No, I am the one who should apologize. I came out of nowhere, right? Name's Mark. I was looking for a nice spot to fish…"

"Suit yourself. This lake is a spot as good as any." He said. "My name is Bartholomeu, but everyone calls me Bart."

"Nice meeting you, Bart." I said.

"Same." He said, minding his own business.

"Well, I will be honest with you Bart." I said. "Actually I have come here to help you with something."

"Help me? With what?" He asked.

"With that pickaxe of yours."

"Wait, how do you know about that? Are you a thief or a griefer?" He asked, annoyed.

"No, none of that, don't worry. It's just that my friend and I want to lend you a hand." I said.

"Who's your friend?" He asked.

"Herobrine." I said.

"Herobrine, the hoax? Yeah, right." He didn't believe me.

"She is right behind that tree, waiting for us. If you want to meet her, fine. But promise me you won't be scared, Bart. She just wants to help you, and so do I."

"A Herobrine that helps people? And it's a she? This is confusing." Bart said.

"It may be confusing, but it's the truth. Come out, Manu." I said.

Manu came out of the trees and walked towards us. Bart seemed unimpressed.

"So what? A girl with white eyes? Even I can arrange that." Bart said.

"But can you do this?" Manu said, raising a block of dirt with the power of her mind.

"Oh gosh. She is really Herobrine!" Bart said, now completely impressed. Even I was impressed! Since when did Herobrine gain the power of levitating blocks around?!

"Like I said Bart, we want to help you. Herobrine's goal in this world

is to help others, not to do any harm."
I said.

"Okay. Come on, let's go back
to my house and we'll talk." Bart said.

Day 11

Back at Bart's house, he explained to us what really happened.

"The guy across the street is called Geoff. We used to be good friends."

"What... street?" Manu whispered.

"Shh!" I said to her. "Please, continue sir."

"Anyway, Geoff was the first one to find diamonds. Granted, he mined them out with an iron pickaxe. Later, he made the first diamond pickaxe and he mined some obsidian. He gave me the obsidian and later, I found some diamonds too. So, with the obsidian provided by Geoff and my own diamonds, I created the first Enchantment Table."

"Right." I said.

"Then Geoff gave me his diamond pickaxe and asked me to enchant it for him. I used my own Experience Points, my own Enchantment table and created a Fortune IV Pickaxe for him, under the condition that we would share it. At first he agreed, but Geoff got more and more attached to that pickaxe as time went by. Eventually, he forbids me from using it and that's when we had a fight."

"I see." Manu said. "So it's like a shared item, right? I mean, each one of you provided some resources – Experience Points from you, pickaxe from him…"

"Don't forget my Enchantment Table." Bart said.

"Yeah, but with obsidian from him…" I said.

"Either way, I have the right to use that pickaxe. I created it! In fact, it should be mine!'

"Where is it now?" Manu asked him.

"With Geoff. I have been asking him to lend it to me but he refuses. That's why I won't let him take any of my crops or my fish."

"We'll talk to him too." I said. "We need to hear both sides of the story before making a move."

Day 12

We knocked at Geoff's house to talk to him.

"Yes?" He said, opening the door.

"Geoff, hi! I am Mark and this is the Herobrine, Manu. We are here to talk to you."

"Is this a joke? Herobrine?" He said.

"No, it's true. Anyway, we are here to help you. Yesterday we talked with Bart."

"Bart?! That liar across the street?" He furiously said.

"What street?!" Manu whispered again.

"Shh!" I replied. "Anyway sir, can we please come in; we just want to talk."

"Sigh. Sure, come in. But I don't have much time; I need to go back to the mine. Not everyone spends all day fishing at ponds and wasting their time." Geoff said.

"Listen, I know you're mad at Bart and you both hate each other right now… But this all seems like it was blown out of proportion." I said. "It's not a big deal, guys. You are adults, come one!"

"Of course not! It's impossible to talk to that child man." Geoff said. "He used MY Diamonds to make MY Diamond Pickaxe. He only had that Enchantment Table because I gave him MY Obsidian! Now I have my own

Enchantment Table so I don't care about his. But this pickaxe is mine!"

"What about his Experience Points?" I asked.

"Not a big deal. I asked for a favor, he did it because he wanted." Geoff said.

"Why don't you share the pickaxe with him?"

"I did! But then he started using it and wouldn't give it back for days. I would ask him, 'where's the pickaxe Bart? I need it for work!' and he would reply like 'Nah, I will give it to you soon...' but it would take days for him to return it!"

"Sigh..." I said. "Come meet us outside the house tomorrow, at noon, Geoff. We'll be leaving you now as to not waste much of your time."

"Uh, okay. I will be there." He said.

Day 13

Manu also asked for Bart to come out at noon. We had both ex-friends outside their respective houses, staring at each other from a distance with anger. Manu and I stood right in the middle, in between both houses.

"This won't be good..." Manu said.

"It's the only way, Manu. Some problems must be tackled face to face. You will never complete this mission unless these two get along." I

said.

"Do you think I can do it?"

"Sure you can. Just be yourself! Let them talk, try to find something they can both agree on." I said. "Bart, Geoff, come over here please."

"Hmpf. I won't talk to that grumpy miner." Bart said.

"Please tell that lazy fisherman that I won't waste my time with him!" Geoff said.

"Guys, please." I said. "You're all grownups. We already know you both shared many items in order to make that pickaxe of yours. In other words, the pickaxe belongs to both of you. Geoff likes to mine more than Bart, but it doesn't give him the right to keep the pickaxe forever."

"Yeah!" Bart said.

"Bart also needs to understand that Geoff is a miner by trade, while Bart is a fisherman/farmer. Therefore Bart spends considerably less time down there in the caves to mine." I said.

"Exactly." Geoff agreed.

"Manu, it's all yours now. Make your move!" I said.

"What? But I don't know how to solve this problem!" She said.

"Just think, Manu. There must be a way of making both of them use the pickaxe in a manner where they are satisfied. Remember you have one wish from the developers."

"Right, the wish... Huh... Think, Manu..." She said. "Oh, oh! Right. Tell me Bart, you don't mine much, right?"

"Correct." He said.

"Okay. At what time of the day do you usually mine?"

"In the morning." Bart replied. "I go out fishing and farming in the afternoon."

"What about you, Geoff?" Manu asked.

"I sleep in the morning and I mine all day and night, since it doesn't matter whether it's sunny or dark down there – you'll always need torches anyway."

"Good! So how about this – since this is such a valuable pickaxe, I will add a new special enchantment to it." Manu said. "Every morning, the pickaxe will be teleported to Bart's inventory where he will be able to use it at will. Every noon, the pickaxe will be teleported to Geoff's inventory and will remain with him for the rest of the day and night. 07:00 am – 12:00 pm for Bart, and 12:01 pm until 06:59 am for Geoff.

What do think?"

"Wait… That sounds reasonable." Bart said.

"Works for me, I guess." Geoff said. "But can you really do that kind of enchantment?"

"Alright. Mark, can I use my wish now?"

"Uh, I guess... That's a brilliant plan, though! Say the words and we'll see if it works. Where's the pickaxe?"

"Here it is." Geoff handed me the pickaxe.

"I wish for the pickaxe to be shared between Bart and Geoff in the periods mentioned before." Manu said.

I snapped my fingers while holding the pickaxe with my left hand. The pickaxe floated away from my hand and flew straight into Geoff's inventory, since it was already past noon.

"Woah! It worked!" Geoff said. "It says here in the pickaxe's description: 'Geoff's pickaxe – Between 12:01 pm to 06:59 am'. This is amazing."

"Now I believe there is no reason to fight over this matter, is there?" Manu asked them.

"No... There isn't." Bart stepped forward and raised his hand.

"Alright, I guess you were right. That was a childish fight. Friends again?" Geoff shook Bart's hand.

"Sure, friends! We really need to go back to sharing items again…"

"Tell me about it, I can't stand eating underground melons anymore." Geoff said.

"Great, it has been settled!" Manu said. "We are now leaving you to it. Good bye!"

"Thank you Herobrine and Mark, life will be much easier for us now." Bart said.

"Thank you to you two!" Geoff said.

"It has been our pleasure, guys."
I said.

Day 14

Manu and I were teleported to the white room.

"Well done, guys." Jeb said. "Manu not only assessed the situation in a proper manner, but she also found the perfect solution to put an end to this. Mark you are a fantastic coach. You guided Manu through all steps and provided her with the perfect solution – to make a compromise."

"He did... I couldn't have

done it without Mark. Thank you so much!" Manu said.

"Oh, come on... It was nothing! Congrats on completing your mission, Manu. I am happy for you!" I said. "I am curious, though – where did that levitation power came from?"

"It's a little something I added a few patch notes ago." Jeb said. "I realized it was hard for Herobrines to be noticed by humans, as most of them did not believe in the Herobrine. So I included this useless but cool little extra ability to convince humans that Herobrine exists."

"Interesting." I said.

"Manu, you have passed the Herobrine Program and you'll be sent back to your world soon. I will talk to Mark first, okay? I will be right there with you." Jeb said.

"Thank you so much! Thank

you too, Mark – come visit me in my server when you have the chance!"

"I will Manu. It was a pleasure working with you. Bye!"

And Manu disappeared.

"Next mission?" Jeb asked me.

"I guess I will continue following the order." I said.

"Good, so Koala it is. Good bye and good luck!" Jeb wished me.

Day 15

My next mission was to help a coward player, Koala, overcome many of his fears in order to become a better player. His next mission seemed easy enough – to rescue a dog from a cave. Easy peasy, right?

I looked around but I couldn't find him. I searched everywhere, but there wasn't anyone in the vicinity. Perhaps Koala already managed to complete the mission and had left the world? No, Jeb wouldn't have sent me down here if that was the case.

I walked for hours searching for Koala or even for any humans living in the area, but to no avail. I was starting to think that Jeb had teleported me to the wrong area. At night, it was hard to see anything so I decided to sleep by a tree.

Day 16

I woke up with some noises coming from under the ground.

"What… is that?" I thought.

Suddenly, I saw a Herobrine coming out of the ground! It was Koala.

"Ah, there you are. I have been looking for you all day." I said.

"Ahhhhh!" He screamed, jumping back into the hole.

"Wait, relax! It's me, Mark. I am Coach Herobrine." I said.

"Coach Herobrine?" He whispered from the hole.

"Yeah. Didn't Jeb tell you about me? I am here to help." I said.

"RRight. Okay, I am coming out." He said, coming out of the hole once more.

"What were you doing down there?" I asked him.

"Well I was hiding from the night monsters."

"You are Herobrine! Hostile mobs do not attack you." I said.

"I know but I don't want to take any chances..." Koala replied.

"How can you destroy and place blocks? I thought Herobrine couldn't do that."

"It has been included in one of the last update." Koala said.

"I should ask Jeb for a list of the new updates for Herobrine...

Anyway, come on Koala. Show me where the player lives, we have to help them."

"Okay, follow me!" He said.

Day 17

Apparently, we were far from the player's house.

"Have you already met the player?" I asked Koala.

"Yeah… I have talked with him but I didn't complete my mission." He said.

"Why were you so far from his house?"

"I was uh… I was trying to find another entrance to the cave, but then it started getting dark and I couldn't proceed because of my fear. Then I hid…"

"It's a rescue mission, right? Involving a dog?" I asked.

"Yes… The dog is not the problem. The cave where he is in is the problem."

"Sure. You hate the dark?" I asked him.

"A lot, sir! Ever since I was little, I was afraid of the dark. I have never gotten over it, though. My mom used to say I would be brave and courageous once I grew up. Look at me now… I am 25 years old and I can't explore a cave by myself because I am too scared!"

"Why can't the player save the dog himself?"

"That particular cave is actually a ravine. The player built his house above the ravine and he was using loads of TNT to blow up some of the ravine's walls. One day, while he was setting up TNTs all over the place, a bunch of Skeletons and Creepers cornered him and he had to run away. Unfortunately the dog didn't follow him and got stuck in a small crevice. Now, his poor dog is down there waiting for the rescue, surrounded by Creepers and TNT blocks ready to explode at any moment. If the human goes down there…"

"Boom." I said.

"Exactly. Herobrine doesn't attract monsters, so I could save him… But…"

"You're afraid of the dark." I said.

"Yes… I know I am a failure. I need to overcome my fears… But it's so hard!"

"I understand you, Koala. Don't worry, that's why I am here." I said.

"Thank you for your support, Mark. Most people mock me… It's good to have someone backing me up."

Day 18

We got to the player's house. Koala knocked at the door and the player came to see us.

"Ah, you're back, Herobrine. And who is this?"

"I am Mark, nice to meet you sir." I said.

"I am Derik, please come in." He said.

"Sorry for not rescuing your puppy yet, Mr. Derik..."

"It's not your fault,

Herobrine. I know this is not an easy mission... It would be much appreciated if you could save Rex from that cave." Derik said.

"Can you show us the entrance to the ravine?" I asked him.

"Sure, it's right through here." We followed Derik into the basement of his house, where he led us to the entrance of the ravine.

"Wow, this is a big ravine!" I said.

"Rex is way down there, to the left. It's impossible to see him from up here. Besides, there is a lot of TNT scattered around and many Creepers lurking the place. I have been trying to pick them off one by one using my bow, but it's impossible in that complete darkness."

"Don't worry, sir. I have come here to provide assistance to Herobrine and we'll figure out a way to rescue Rex." I said. "I only ask you to stay behind, as you could alert the Creepers and other mobs."

"Absolutely. Thank you for your help." Derik said. "I can't wait to see my pup again!"

Koala and I got down into the ravine and searched for a good area to start our mission. Koala was shaking, even though I was holding a torch and lighting the way.

"Relax, Koala. This will be easy and quick."

"I don't know, Mr. Mark. I am afraid of the dark and I can't see anything other than the torch!"

Despite my words of encouragement to him, I knew convincing this guy to complete the mission was not going to be easy.

Day 19

Down there at the ravine, Koala and I were trying to find a way to save Rex, Derik's loyal (but stranded) dog.

"I know you really like Pandas and Bamboos, but why is that?" I asked him.

"Oh, most people say that. It's just that Koalas were never introduced in the base game, and since Pandas kinda look like Koalas…" He said.

"Still, that makes zero sense." I said.

"Well, I suppose some nicknames don't make sense, but that's how my friends used to call me." Koala

387

said. "Now please Mr. Mark, don't stop lighting the way down! I can't be in the dark for too long."

"Relax. I have brought some extra torches from Derik and I will be placing them all the way down." I said.

We continued walking and exploring the ravine. Once we reached the bottom we saw some TNT blocks on the walls and even on the ground.

"Look, TNT! Careful, we don't want to blow things up on accident." I said.

But as we progressed through the cave, more and more TNT popped up everywhere there were some 100 or more TNT blocks scattered all over the ravine. A frightening, uneasy sight.

"There's too many TNT blocks here…" Koala said.

"Can you see the dog?" I asked him.

"No… I can barely see three meters ahead of us!" Koala said. "Please sir, place more torches on the walls!"

"I am lighting this place up as much as I can, Koala." I said.

Day 20

We explored the ravine and didn't find any signs of the dog.

"Here, here, Rex, where are you?" I called for him.

"Here boy, come out from wherever you are!" Koala said.

"He must be even deeper down the ravine. Poor dog must have gotten hungry and went after some food sources – Zombie meat is the only possible source down here." I said.

"Oh no! I hate Zombies!" Koala said.

"Is there anything you don't hate?" I jokingly asked him.

"Uhh… Pandas!" Koala replied.

We continued searching for Rex until we finally heard him barking far away into a dark crevice.

"He's down there! We need to take him out." I said.

"BBut it's extra dark down there!" Koala said.

"Listen Koala, you turned into Herobrine because you were too afraid of the dark, and this fear must have caused some sort of trouble for other people around you." I said. "This is your chance to overcome your fear, and to prove yourself to Jeb."

"I know sir, but…" Koala said.

"Here's the thing, Koala. Everyone's afraid of something. I am afraid of monsters when I am in my normal human form. I am afraid of Illagers, and also of the Wither. There are so many things that I am afraid of, that I can't even remember. But you know why I am not afraid of the dark?"

"Why?" He asked me.

"Cause the dark is just the lack of light. I know not being able to see where you're stepping or walking may be strangely scary, but there is no need to be afraid of something so trivial. You'll be facing the dark every night for the rest of your life, so you might as well get used to it. Don't you think that would be a good idea?" I asked him.

"Yes... I understand what you mean, but I... I can't get myself to..."

"That's the problem, Koala. Please, don't use these words: 'can't, won't, couldn't'... Be positive. Think positive. Go the other way around – you can do it! You should do it! You'll become a better person in the end." I said.

"Thank you, Mr. Mark. That is very inspiring. I am tired of leaving in fear of everything! I want to… I want to explore the world! I never did it because my fear was always taking over me… But, but… I can do it!"

"Exactly!" I said.

"I can do it!" He repeated.

"Now that you're inspired, take the first step down that crevice. Don't think about the dark, Koala. Just do it. Think of your objective – we got a dog to rescue!" I said.

"Okay!" Koala said, stepping down into the crevice. He continued walking without saying a word for a few seconds.

"Keep it up. You're doing great." I said, coming from behind him. However, I lost track of Koala soon after. I placed some torches but it was too dark down there to see anything. For a moment, I thought Koala had fallen into another hole.

"Koala? Where are you?" I asked. He didn't reply.

I could hear Rex barking in the distance, but no signs of Koala. I continued going down and placing more torches, thinking that maybe Koala could have hidden somewhere because he was scared again. Then, I saw Rex right in front of me – Koala was holding him.

"Hey, I found him!" Koala said.

" Woah, that was impressive!" I said. "You just went down there in complete darkness and retrieved the dog?" I asked him.

"Well, yeah, when you put it that way…" He said. "To be honest, I wasn't thinking of anything while down there. The only thing I had in mind was to save this cute puppy!"

"Congratulations Koala! Let's go back, Derik will be so delighted." I said.

Day 21

Upon returning, Derik couldn't stop thanking us for retrieving his dog. He even wanted to give us a reward and offered some ores, but we refused. The job of a Herobrine comes free of charge!

Back at the white room, Jeb seemed proud of Koala's victory.

"I am so happy to see a man overcoming his fears." Jeb said. "What is even more impressive – you completed this task without even using any wish!"

"Thank you Mr. Jeb. However, I still have many other fears!" He said.

"We all do, Koala. We all do. The secret is to never let your fears run your life." Jeb said. "Since you didn't use any wishes, you won't have to complete any other tasks from now on."

"That's great!" Koala said.

"Thank you once again for the guidance, Mark. The more time you spend down there with the Herobrines, the happier I feel about picking you for the job." Jeb said.

"Oh, it's an honor Jeb! My pleasure." I said.

"Koala, I will be speaking to you soon. You will be dismissed from your role as Herobrine. Well done!" Jeb said.

"Thank you Mr. Jeb, and

thank you too Mr. Mark! I will never forget how much you helped me!" Koala said.

"Thank you, Koala. It was really fun completing this mission with you! Good bye!"

Koala disappeared and Jeb asked me about my next mission.

"Keeping the order, Jeb. I want to face a bigger challenge now!" I said.

"Okay. The 3rd mission is indeed a challenge; it's definitely the second hardest mission of all six Herobrines. Good luck, and see you soon!" Jeb said, snapping his fingers.

Day 22

I woke up inside a small wooden house. Seemed dirty and abandoned, so I got up and left the house. Some of the walls were missing and the door was gone.

"Someone must have left this house a very long time ago." I said.

Once outside, I saw two other houses in a similar fashion — abandoned, destroyed, and unfit for a decent living. No signs of recent human activity in the area.

"What is this, an abandoned village?" I thought.

Walking around the area, I couldn't find any clues as to what had happened to the place. Therefore, I figured the best course of action would be to leave the place and look for my next person to mentor – Parson, the 3rd Herobrine.

Day 23

Finding Parson was not as easy as expected. The fact that Jeb teleported me to an abandoned village in the middle of nowhere must have some importance to this quest, but I was still wondering what exactly it meant.

I followed a dirt trail leading to a large river, but there was no one around. I stopped for a moment and decided to drink some water. As I kneeled down to drink from the river, a voice came from behind.

"Stop right there. You cannot do that." The voice said.

"Pardon me? I am thirsty." I said.

"This is my river, now get out!" I turned around and I saw a Herobrine standing right behind me. "Oh, sorry lad. I thought you were one of those slinky Villagers."

"What? Why would you think that? I don't even look like a Villager!" I said.

"Well, you never know what tricks they might pull on ya." He said. "Name's Parson, nice to meet ya."

"Yeah, and I am Mark. I have come here to help you." I said.

"Good, good. Jeb did tell me that help was on the way, but it took you longer than I expected." He said.

"Sorry, I was busy helping other Herobrines." I said.

"So I heard. Come on, stop by my house and we'll talk. Don't let those stinky Villagers see ya." He said, rushing me to his house.

"What? Why are you so scared of the Villagers? They are peaceful creatures!" I said.

"Don't care, doesn't matter. Let's go." He said.

Day 24

At Parson's house, I wanted to know why he was acting so strange.

"Why do you keep insulting Villagers?" I asked him. "Also, how come you have your own house? Herobrines don't have houses."

"Well, ya know; I figured, since I was going to spend some time down here in this forsaken land, I might as well be comfortable, ya know? Don't want to live at large, running from one bush to another and eating grass from the ground. We're still humans by heart."

"Uh… Okay." I said.

"Villagers, the real freaking villains." Parson said. "Bunch of stinky losers."

"Right…" I said, confused. "What do you have against them?"

"They're the ones who are causing trouble." Parson said. "If it wasn't for 'em, I would have completed my mission a long time ago and would be out of here. It's been over 10 days… I don't want to be a Herobrine any longer. The worst thing is, I only have two more weeks before I am kicked out and banned for good by Jeb."

"What are the Villagers doing?" I asked him.

"They're running amok, wreaking havoc." Parson said. "They're grieving a human Village."

"Really?! I had never seen that!" I said.

"Right. I can take you there to take a look. But be careful, those are

404

real smart stinky creatures." Parson said. "I got a little too close the other day and almost had to kiss my Herobrine form goodbye, because they kicked the heck out of me."

"Sure... Please let me have a look and analyze the situation." I said.

Day 25

Parson took me to see for myself what the 'Villagers' were doing to the humans. Personally, I had never heard of a case where Villagers attacked a group of humans. In the original report, Jeb told me that Illagers attacked them; but after hearing Parson's report, I was confused.

The human village was not far from Parson's house. We climbed a nearby tree and stood there on watch, only to see a village surrounded by Illagers. The humans inside were building walls, fences and trying to keep the Illagers outside.

"Oh, so they really are Illagers like Jeb said!" I said. "They're not Villagers, Parson. You got me confused for a moment."

"Villagers, Illagers, who cares. They're all the same to me. Bunch of stinky lads." Parson said.

"Hey, of course not! They are definitely not the same. Perhaps same family, but Villagers are friendly while Illagers are not."

"Same thing, bud. Now, tell me – any idea on how to tackle this issue?" Parson asked me.

"Not really. We should be careful, since they are hostile towards pretty much any living creature in the world. Including Herobrines, of course."

"Tell me about it." Parson said, showing me some scars in his arm. "Let's go back. Won't be of any help to waste our time here and do nothing all day."

Day 26

Back at Parson's house, we discussed all day the best way to fight the Illagers. There were only two of us and at the very least 50 of them. Illagers can be pretty strong, and even a strong Herobrine or two won't be able to take them down.

Parson mentioned the wish and asked me if we could use it to get rid of all Illagers, or simply teleport them far away. Since I was out of ideas, we did try it to see for ourselves…

"Okay, I am ready." I said.

"Right. I wish for the Illagers to disappear." Parson said out loud.

Immediately, I received a notification on my feed: INVALID REQUEST.

"Oh my... It didn't work." I said.

"Alright, then I wish for all Illagers to be defeated by a huge Zombie." Parson said.

"Again, it was not possible." I said.

"Heck, what's the use of a wish if you can't have what you want?" Parson said.

"Sorry, You can't use the wish to complete the mission for you. It is only for assisting you in your mission." I said.

"I will have to think about it..." Parson said.

Day 27

Another day went by, and Parson and I still didn't have any idea on how to proceed.

"Do the Illagers stay there at all times, surrounding that poor village?" I asked him.

"No. They leave for a couple hours every now and then. When they do, the humans take that opportunity to reinforce the outside walls and even plant some traps. It's all useless, though – the Illagers are a smart bunch." Parson says. "They deactivate all traps with the help of a magic user of some sorts. A wizard, if you may call it so."

"Impressive." I said. "Have you already talked to the humans inside the village?" I asked.

"No, can't do." He said. "Poor lads are stuck in there; they won't stop working for a minute. I guess they haven't even spotted me yet amidst that ocean of Villagers."

"Illagers." I corrected him.

"Same thing." Parson said. "Anyway, we have to find a way to help them."

"What about finding a way THROUGH them?" I asked Parson.

"Excuse me? I don't know if I am following you." Parson said.

"Let's dig an underground tunnel leading up to the Village. Let's go talk to them and see how we can help." I said.

"Brilliant idea, lad. Once they see Herobrine coming out of an

412

underground hole, how do you think they are going to react?" Parson said.

"The reaction is, most of the time, negative and hostile." I said. "I should know, because I was a Herobrine once. However this is an expected behavior and it should not deter you from trying to do your job. If they're hostile towards you, walk your way around that. Find a solution, think through it."

"Wow. You really like a Coach Herobrine, aren't ya?" Parson said. "Well, color me impressed Mr. Mark. You convinced me. Let's go get them."

"Let's go!" I said.

Day 28

We started digging a hole which would take us right into the middle of the human village. Our goal was to assist the humans. It was impossible to reach them because of the Illager horde outside their walls.

"All right, lead the way Parson! I will be right behind you." I said.

"Well lad, tell me something – you're the one who came up with the idea, shouldn't you be the one digging the hole?"

"I am here to help you complete the mission, Parson. I can't take the lead on all decisions, though."

"Fair enough. I wouldn't want you to take all the credit once we finish the job. I want to be free from this role as soon as possible, so let me get started here." Parson said, digging the hole.

He continued digging for some minutes.

"Did you memorize how many blocks away we were?" I asked him.

"Yeah, of course. Sure thing." Parson said. "We should be under their feet in just a few minutes."

"I will trust you, Parson. Just make sure we don't get out right next to the Illagers." I said.

Day 29

Parson was recounting the tunnel blocks and making sure we were under the right spot before emerging from below.

"Right, this should do it." He said. "Ready?"

"Always ready." I replied.

"Here we go!" Parson opened the last block above us and got out of the tunnel. I followed him. The sun was bright and we were both blinded by it, after staying inside that tunnel for hours. As we recovered our vision, we saw three armed humans pointing bows at us.

"Invaders!" One of them said.

"Please, calm down." I said. "We are here to…"

"Listen, I am Herobrine so stop with the threats already." Parson interrupted me.

"Herobrine?! What a joker!" The other player said. "Come on, we'll take you two as prisoners! We don't have time to waste with thieves."

"No, you got it all wrong. We are not thie" I was interrupted by the players pushing us away.

"Move! You'll both stay inside the cells." The player said.

"You don't get it, do you, lads?" Parson said. "Look at me. I am Herobrine!" He used his powers to levitate some buckets lying on the

ground.

"Impossible! This thief is indeed Herobrine! We need to lock them up and make sure they don't come out until we are safe!" The other player said.

"But, come on gentlemen…" I was trying to defuse the situation, but Parson was definitely not a calm person to deal with others. We were locked up in a cell guarded by one single guard outside.

Day 30

Before we could explain to everyone our current objectives to help them, Parson and I were locked away in a cell and treated like a pair of common thieves.

Despite Parson trying to prove himself as Herobrine (an attempt which he did poorly and at the wrong time), the players ignored our identity and threw us into their cells.

"Now stay there because we have got to deal with a bigger threat!" The other players said.

They were too busy dealing with the Illagers and completely ignored our

419

desire to help them. Helping Parson with this mission is going to be harder than I imagined. Mostly because Parson is not a people's person and he always speaks his mind without giving it a second thought.

Before trying to help these people in their battle against the Illagers, I must find a way to teach Parson how to deal with daily situations! It's impossible to tell whether (or when) the Illagers will break into the Village, so we need to get this over with as soon as possible!

Book 5: Not An Easy Job

Day 1

I am imprisoned with Parson in a village inhabited by humans... We have come here to help these people and now we are their prisoners! I swear I have seen this happen before somewhere... But that is not important right now.

The most important thing to do is: teach Parson how to deal with people! His arrogant behavior is causing conflicts. Either he changes the way he acts, or we are doomed! Another important thing we need to do is convince these good people to let us out.

I always knew this task was going to be quite intimidating, moderately hard to say the least. But it's proving to be harder and harder by the day… I should not ignore Jeb's evaluation of all missions before accepting them! This is indeed one of the hardest ones.

Day 2

The guards outside were screaming and shouting trying to keep the Illagers away while fencing up their feeble and heavily damaged walls. I have come up with a good plan so that they will free us from the prison.

"Yes, keep it up, silly humans." Parson said. "This whole village is coming down, and it's because you ignored our help!" He shouted as if the guards could hear us from where we were.

"Don't say that, Parson." I said. "Remember we are both

humans, too."

"I know. But we are not dumb like those people!" He said.

"Listen, Parson." I said. "As Herobrine, there is something very important to learn. Dealing with people is not as easy as it seems. Especially you, who always looks down on people and treats them badly."

"What? I don't do that. It's just that I am smarter than the average human." Parson said.

"That's the problem, right there." I said. "What's the point in bragging about being 'smarter' than others? That sounds silly and superfluous. Don't be like that, Parson. People will avoid you if you do."

"Sigh." Parson didn't want to agree with what I was telling him. "Fine. Let's just pretend that you are

right. Then what?"

"Listen to them. Sometimes, it's more important to listen to what they have to say than to open your mouth first." I said.

"Noted. Since we are locked down here, how are we supposed to listen to what they have to say?" Parson asked me.

"Well… In this case we can't do that. So we try to find a way to bring them here. We need to talk, and remember – be patient. Last time, you blew everything up because you weren't patient enough."

"But I am the Herobrine of this server! I wasn't lying." He said.

"I am not asking you to lie. I am asking you to tell it in a nice and respectful way."

"Then teach me how to do it, oh mighty teacher of Herobrines."

Parson mocked me.

"You jest, but let me show you. Instead of coming out of the hole and saying 'hey look at me, I am Herobrine.

I can make things float!' like crazy, you can do it differently. You could have said 'Hello, I am sorry for breaking into your village, but there is something important that I need to tell you. I have come to assist you with the Illagers. How can I be of your service?' or something along those lines."

"Hmm. Okay." Parson said.

"Note how I worded what you have to say to them. It is much friendlier." I said. "If we managed to talk to them like that in the first place, perhaps we would be outside by now helping them fend off the Illagers."

"Alright. You win. I know I am stubborn and all, but there is no need to shove it all over my face." Parson said. "I need to help these people before my time as Herobrine is over."

"That's the spirit, Parson. We will help them!" I said.

Day 3

As time passed by, no guards came down to check on us. We need to talk to at least one of them in order to convince them of our good intentions.

"It has been 3 days and no one has come here." Parson said.

"I know… I believe they're having a hard time fighting those Illagers, so they don't have time to come down here." I said.

"How are we going to help them if they don't even talk to us?"

Parson asked me.

"Patience is a virtue, my friend."
I said. "We'll wait a little longer."

"And then what?" He asked me.

"Then, we might have to go for
Plan B."

"Wait, we have a Plan B?"
Parson was surprised. "What is Plan
B?"

"Plan B is 'forget everything I
said and do whatever it takes to get the
job done'". I said.

Day 4

Four days and still no guards went down to check on us. We could no longer sit and wait.

"That's it. We're going with Plan B." I said.

"Right, but what do you mean with 'forget everything you said'?" Parson asked me.

"Help me break these bars. They're made of Obsidian, but we have the ability to break some blocks now." I said.

"What? But we are escaping prison! They will be mad at us!" Parson said.

"That's what I meant with Plan B. Sometimes, Parson, you have to leave the chatter behind and proceed with some drastic actions. This is one of those moments. We need be out there as soon as possible, before the village is invaded by Illagers.

We destroyed the bars and escaped the prison. Once we stepped outside, we witnessed a war scene: guards everywhere, placing blocks and fortifying the walls while angry Illagers tried to jump across the fortification.

"More blocks to the East side!" A guard shouted.

"More blocks here, in the South!" A group of guards asked from the other side.

"That guy up there giving the orders must be the leader. Let's go talk to him." I said. "By the way Parson, you'll do the talking. Remember what I told you about being patient and also about Plan B – How you need to act fast when there is no other choice."

"Okay... I will try." Parson said.

We approached the guard from behind and Parson touched his shoulder. The guard turned around and was instantly scared by the sight.

"My molly! Herobrine escaped!" He shouted.

"Listen, bud I mean, sir." Parson said. "I am here to help. Please, let me assist you against the Illagers."

"No! You are lying! I will send you back to prison right away! Where are the other guards?!"

"Sir, this is serious! Your village is about to go down. There are Illagers everywhere, and they're inches away from invading the whole place. They'll run this village to the ground. Now, you either accept my help or accept

your doom. Stop wasting our time!"
Parson gave him an ultimatum.

"Okay…" The guard said.
"Okay. If you want to help, go ahead!
But don't disturb our job!"

"By the way, remember I can
grant you one wish." I told Parson.
"You can use this wish to protect the
village from the enemy."

"Hmm… A wish, huh?" Parson
pondered.

"Exactly. Do you have anything
in mind?"

"In fact I do. I wish for
impenetrable and huge walls around
the village." Parson said.

"Your wish is my command!" I
snapped my fingers and the walls
turned into Obsidian instantly, rising 30
meters from the ground. The village
was now safe from the invaders, who
would never be able to tear the wall
down!

"What just… What is…" The guard watching us was speechless.

"Impressive. This should definitely do the job." Parson said.

"Good thinking, Parson!" I said.

"Our village is safe! Thank you so much to both of you!" The guard said.

"You can thank us later. Now let's go talk to everyone, shall we?" Parson said, tapping the guard in the shoulder. I was impressed by his decision making and his behavior. It was not exactly as friendly as I pictured, but Parson was getting

much better at this job!

Day 5

Vall, the guard leader, called all guards and other human villagers to come meet us at the square.

"Everyone, this is Herobrine and his assistant. Believe it or not, but Herobrine is the one who made that huge wall. We are now safe from the enemy!" Vall said, cheering.

All other humans clapped and cheered along him.

"Herobrine, why did you come here to help us?" Vall asked Parson.

"Because that's my job. I help

people all over the world." Parson said. "But you guys wouldn't listen to us… And you locked us up in that cell without hesitation."

"We sincerely apologize. I wish there was a way to compensate for our error." Vall said.

"It's okay, Vall." I said. "There is no need to do that; however, I would like to say our mission here is yet over."

"Wait, what?!" Parson was surprised. He thought it was all over.

"That's right. Our next goal is to drive all Illagers away from the area. Yes, we are safe inside these walls and they are impenetrable. However, the enemy lies behind our defenses. Leaving the village is not safe, and it could be dangerous for anyone trying to explore the surroundings."

"I thought my mission was over…" Parson told me.

"If it was over, Jeb would have teleported us both back to his base." I said. "We need to finish this once and for all."

"Alright." Parson said. "We'll get rid of all Illagers for you!" He told the humans.

They cheered once again. I looked at Parson and he nodded – I knew he had no idea how to get rid of the Illagers, and neither did I. The humans had already used their only wish, and now we would have to do everything on our own.

Day 6

Parson and I had a hard mission ahead of us – defeating all Illagers and keeping the village safe.

"This won't be easy at all..." Parson said.

"I know. Jeb already said that Illagers attack Herobrines, so that also includes me." I said.

"What if we build a big pit, lure all Illagers into it and then close it?" Parson asked me.

"Illagers would never run into a pit, Parson. They are much smarter than the average hostile mob."

"Then what if we asked the guards to use their Bows to take the Illagers down, one by one? They could climb atop the new wall and shoot arrows!"

"Illagers also have Archers, Parson. In fact, they use their powerful crossbows which are even more dangerous than a normal bow! We can't risk the guard's well-being." I said.

"Darn it. I am out of ideas..." Parson said.

"Don't give up just now, Parson." I said. "I should say you are doing a fantastic progress. You don't even look like the same Parson I met a few days ago!"

"Well... Thanks." He said.

"Your ideas were good. Unfortunately we can't use them, but you're on the right path. Sometimes when we are trying to come up with the perfect plan, we have to think of all possibilities." I said.

"All possibilities, uh…" Parson repeated. "I might have a new plan for us."

Day 7

Parson didn't tell me what his plan was about, but I trust him.

"Follow me, Mark." He said.

"Right behind you." I told him.

Parson and I went all the way up the front wall through the stairs. Up there, we took a brief look over the area, before the Illagers could notice us and point their crossbows at our heads.

"Interesting. There are a LOT of Illagers." Parson said.

"Indeed. It seems there's even more than before." I said.

"Then, this plan will be perfect!" Parson seemed content with his idea. "Now let's go down there because I need to test something, and you'll help me."

"Alright."

Once down, Parson picked up a Cobblestone block and placed it on the ground.

"Now, get on the block, Mark." He asked me.

"Uh, okay. What do you want to do?" I asked him.

"I'll try to levitate the block with you standing on it." He said.

"What for?"

"It's part of my plan. Now let's try it out!" Parson used his telekinesis powers on the block and, surprisingly enough, it worked! He levitated the block with me on it.

"Awesome!" I said.

"Let me see how far I can take you. Stand still, Mark!" He told me.

"Alright, just don't do anything silly!" I said.

He lifted the block all the way to the sky, close to the wall. Once I was in the same height as the top of the front wall, he asked me to step out of the block and stand on the wall. I did it without much hassle.

"Fantastic. My portable elevator worked!" Parson said.

"That was indeed impressive." I said to myself. "I guess you took my advice of 'all possibilities' seriously, huh." I shouted from the top of the wall.

"Yep! Now get down here because we need to prepare for my plan." Parson shouted back.

Day 8

Now that Parson had already tested his 'elevator', it was time to proceed with his so-called plan.

"What's on your mind, Parson?" I asked him.

"First, we'll have to tell all humans to climb the walls. Once everyone is up there, we'll open the gates."

"What?"

"Yes. Will attract the Illagers to go inside the village. Once all Illagers are inside the village, we'll close the gate and create a ladder to jump off to the other side of the wall. The humans

443

can then live in peace, with all Illagers locked inside the wall forever."

"There are two things about this plan that are too crazy to consider. One, do you intend to use one of the humans as bait? That's too dangerous!"

"Well, it's the only way to attract the Illagers." Parson said.

"And two… Well… We're talking about forcing the humans to abandon their village! I mean, their place is not that big but still it's their home!"

"I know. The problem is that there are too many Illagers outside. I'd say some 200 Illagers or more, as you saw for yourself."

"Yes… I have no idea where they came from." I said.

"We can't defeat them. The humans can't, either. This is our best shot." Parson said.

"Alright. I see you've got a plan. Let's talk to the leader of the village, Vall, and reveal your plan to him. We need their approval before proceeding."

"Fair enough. Let's go." Parson said.

Day 9

Parson and I met with Vall to discuss the plan with him.

"Listen, we have got some bad news and good news." Parson said.

"Bad news first." Vall said.

"Well, Mark and I can't beat those Illagers. There are too many of them and we can't do it, even with your help." Parson revealed.

"Ah. I figured." Vall said. "When you said you two were going to beat them up all by yourselves, I truly doubted it. There's an Illager army out there, they're by the hundreds and we barely have 50 humans living here!"

"Correct. And the good news is… We have a plan." Parson said.

"That's great, would love to hear it!" Vall asked us.

"Psst…" I whispered to Parson. "Are you sure the plan is the 'good news'? I mean, we are talking about abandoning the village! This sounds more like a 'double bad news' deal to me!"

"Relax, Mark. I am sure we can convince them of doing it. Remember what you said, you can always resolve a problem by talking." Parson said.

"Well, we need to try." I said.

"Very well, Vall. The plan may not be as easy or comforting as it sounds. In fact, you would have to abandon your village and leave it behind in order to protect all humans who live here. I believe this is a fair tradeoff." Parson concluded.

"I understand…" Vall said, analyzing our plan. "If it's for the protection of my citizens, I am willing to do whatever it takes. Plus, the village is already damaged because of all the previous attacks. It would take us as much time to repair it than to build a new one elsewhere."

"Great." Parson said.

"Uh… That went unexpectedly well." I said.

"Just tell us what we need to do and we'll follow your plan." Vall said.

"Okay. Please ask all humans to take all of their belongings – items in chests, goods, valuable possessions, etc. Tomorrow, we'll leave this village for good."

Day 10

Today everyone was ready to carry on with Parson's plan.

"We are all here, Herobrine." Vall said. "Now what?"

"Tell them to take the stairs and climb to the top of the front wall. When they are on top of the wall they must be still and be in a crouching position. I repeat – stay crouched at the top of the wall! We don't want to draw attention from the Illagers just yet."

"Okay, I'll ask them to do what you asked." Vall said.

"What about the two of us?" I asked Parson.

"Now I will need to ask a guard to take the role of bait..." Parson said.

"No! It's too dangerous for them, Parson." I said. "Please take me instead. I can be the bait for the plan."

"Well, okay." He said. "Step on that cobblestone block in the middle of the village."

"Okay, then what?"

"Then, I will climb to the top of the front wall along with the other humans. Once there, I'll tell Vall to open the gates using the main lever which is up there. You'll stand still to attract the Illagers inside. Once they get close, I will lift the block and take you out of there, safe and sound. Then, Vall closes the gates and the Illagers will be trapped forever."

"Gee... It does sound like a good plan, but it's also dangerous..." I said.

"Trust me, I got you." Parson said.

"Okay. Just don't let me fall!" I said, standing on the block. Parson went up and stayed in position.

"Vall, open the gates." He asked.

"Gates are now opening!" Vall shouted.

As soon as the main gate opened, a horde of Illagers ran inside towards me. I could see their penetrating eyes from the distance, angry and ready to attack me with all their might. At that moment, all alone in that village, I knew I was completely and utterly powerless against that many enemies – facing them off was not an option, and neither was running away.

"Parson!" I shouted.

The Illagers were getting closer and closer. I could almost feel their heavy breathing.

"Ready!" Parson said, lifting the block and taking me up in the sky along with it.

"Phew... That was REALLY close!" I said, holding onto the block and watching all the angry Illagers running around in circles below.

"Now I will bring you here." Parson said. "Are all Illagers inside?"

"Yes!" Vall replied.

"Then, close the gates." Parson ordered.

"Closing the gates!" Vall shouted. Now, the human village was no more – it had become a new home for the Illagers instead.

As the block approached the front wall, I accidentally slipped away and fell down. Luckily, I managed to grab onto the block with my right hand, but I was now dangling from the floating block!

"Oh my gosh!" Parson screamed.

"Please, take me out of here!" I begged him. "I am going to fall down! I can't hold for long!"

"Hold tight!" Parson said, trying to concentrate on his Telekinesis power. The block was getting closer to the front wall, but my hand was giving away. I tried to hold with both hands; however, the left one couldn't reach the top of the block. I was wasting my energy trying to hold with both, so I decided to hold still with only my right hand.

"Just a few more meters..." Parson shouted.

"Please... Hurry!" I said, as my hand hurt.

At some point, I literally couldn't hold it for any longer. My hand let go of the block and I fell down... Right onto the top of the front wall, next to Parson!

"Phew... That was really close." Parson said.

"Ugh... My hand hurts..." I said.

"I am sorry, Mark. I didn't think it would be so dangerous... In my mind, the plan was perfect." He apologized to me.

"Not your fault, Parson." I said. "In fact, I am the one who slipped. I wasn't paying attention. The Illagers distracted me back there."

"Well, good thing you're safe and sound now." Parson said.

"You're lucky for not falling down there!" Vall said. "If you had fallen... We would never be able to retrieve you from the hands of those monsters!"

"If I had fallen, most likely I would be defeated by the Illagers and teleported back to Jeb..." I whispered to Parson. "But I don't want to leave my job with a bad record. I want to help every single Herobrine in this world!"

"Good for us, Herobrines." Parson said.

"Parson, the plan was perfect after all!" I said. "The Illagers are locked up for good."

"Now what, Mr. Herobrine?" Vall asked him.

"Now, tell the humans to build

a ladder. Let's get out of here to the other side of the wall. We are now free!" He said.

Day 11

After building the ladder, everyone climbed down from the top of the wall.

"Thank heavens." Vall shouted. "I don't recall the last time I stepped outside the walls of our village. It feels good to be free!"

All the other humans cheered and celebrated. It seemed that losing their entire village was not a problem – freedom was the best thing from this tradeoff!

"Now, you can build your next village anywhere you want." Parson said. "Remember to make some extra thick walls, just in case, you know."

456

"Absolutely." Vall said. "Now that we have the time, we'll make the biggest, best village anyone has ever seen! Also, we'll add some extra layers of wall to fend off the entrance to the old village – we don't want anyone meddling around that area."

"Sounds like a good idea." I said.

"Our mission here is finally complete. Isn't it?" Parson asked me.

"Indeed. You have completed your goal, Parson!" I said.

"Thank you so much for the help, Herobrine!" Vall said. "On behalf of all the people in my village, we are thankful for your assistance and we'll be glad to have you back anytime you want."

"You're welcome sir. I am glad to know my work was useful to you." Parson said. "It wouldn't be possible without the help and guidance of my trusted friend, Mark."

"Glad to help!" I said.

We shook hands with Vall, said goodbye to all the people of the village and left the area.

"Now what?" Parson asked me.

"Let's go rest for a bit. Jeb should teleport us back to his headquarters anytime soon." I said.

Day 12

Today, I was once again in the white room all by myself. Parson was nowhere to be seen.

"Welcome back." Jeb said, standing behind me.

"Oh hey!" I replied. "Where's Parson?"

"He has returned to his home." Jeb said. "He didn't want to wake you up, so he asked me to wish you the best. He also asked you to pay him a visit one of these days."

"Oh, I see. Absolutely, I will!" I said.

"As with all other previous Herobrines, I will provide you with a detailed list of their server addresses and precise location. Now, Mr. Mark, the Herobrine Coach, what do you think of your last mission?"

"It was... thrilling, to say the least." I said. "As you had warned me, it was one of the hardest missions of all six. Honestly, I thought I would have a hard time teaching Parson how to behave as Herobrine. However, I was wrong – assisting him was the easiest of all tasks. The real challenge was figuring out and conducting the perfect plan to help the stranded villagers."

"I see. What I really liked about this mission is that you provided great input and taught Parson really well. From then on, Parson took most of the steps and decisions by himself in order to solve

his quest. Well done!" Jeb said.

"Thank you."

"For your next mission, what would it be?" Jeb asked me.

"As per usual, I will go with the same order as before." I said.

"Sounds good. I will be teleporting you to Lara's server now. She has already failed her two previous jobs. The third and last job is to help her own friends and also get redemption from her mistakes."

"Sounds tough, but I suppose I can handle it." I said.

"Good luck and I will be waiting for you here." Jeb said.

"Bye! See you soon!" I said.

Day 13

I was teleported back to the Overworld. This time, there were four houses in front of me.

"Uh, not bad. It will be much easier to find my next objective." I said.

I roamed around each one of the four houses. No one was there.

"Hello?" I said. "Is anyone in there?"

I stopped by one of the houses and looked inside from the window. Everything was organized and the house was also very clean. It looked like someone had been tidying it up for a while, even though there was no one there.

The same with the other three houses – no one inside, but all clean and in order. I had no idea what was going on.

"Strange... It's as if these people have just left their houses to go somewhere. But where...? Are these the same friends who had gone to the Nether and got lost in there?" I thought to myself.

Then, I heard someone crying nearby, behind a tree. I walked up on them and saw a Herobrine girl sitting by the tree.

"Uh, hello there." I said.

"Oh! What?!" She quickly got on her feet and stopped crying, wiping the tears from her face."

"Sorry to scare you." I said.

"No, I… I wasn't scared by you! It's just that… I didn't hear anyone coming by." She said.

"Are you Lara?" I asked her.

"Yes… Please, go away! I don't want to see anyone… I have already let other people down. I don't want to do it again!" She said, running away from me.

"Wait, please!" I said, but the girl ignored my pleas.

Now, I had to chase the girl and explain to her who I was!

Day 14

I had been looking all day for Lara, but to no avail. She wasn't hiding in any of the four houses and she wasn't in the nearby forest, where I first met her.

"This girl is only making my job harder... I am here to help her!" I thought.

I stopped in the middle of the small village and decided to prepare lunch. I had found some apples and wheat, so I lit up a small campfire to cook them. And then, someone tapped me on the shoulder from

behind. It was Lara!

"Oh, hey, you are back!" I said.

"Yes... Sorry for running away from you." She said. "It's just that I am very upset these days... I can't do anything right!"

"Sit down by the fire, will ya?" I asked her. "Let's talk.

She sat next to me and I cooked the wheat into bread. We shared the bread and I wanted to know more about her story.

"I am Mark, the Herobrine Coach." I said.

"Yeah... I kind of figured it out when you first came by." She said.

"Good! So you know I am here to help you, right?"

"Yes. But no one can help me... I am a lost case." She said.

"Don't say that. Everyone can be helped. You just have to accept the help." I said.

"Okay... I do accept your help, then." She said.

"It's easier said than done." I said. "Just saying you do accept my help is not enough. You'll also have to act upon it – you will have to follow some of my orders, you will have to listen to my advices, and you will also have to take action in order to complete your mission. Are you ready for that?"

"Yes… I suppose." She said.

"Great! Then I can assure you that you can do this and it will not be as hard as you think." I said.

Day 15

Today, I asked Lara about the houses and her story.

"So, what's up with these four houses? How come they're so clean?"

"These are the houses of my friends and mine." She said. "Mine is that yellow one.

"Cool!"

"I am the one who have been cleaning them up." She said.

"So, tell me your story, Lara." I asked her.

"I would rather not..." She replied.

"I know revisiting the past isn't always easy. I am aware you might feel guilty. However, trust me – this is the best way to redeem yourself from your mistakes. You must tackle them head on!"

"Okay…" She said. "The four of us used to live here in peace. I really liked my friends. They were always there for me… But I was always an insecure person. I have always been like that. Then one day…" She shivered.

"Please, continue." I calmly asked her.

"Then one day, Joe said he wanted to go to the Nether. He was always the one to come up with plans and whatnot. I said I didn't want to, because I wasn't ready. I was always scared of going to the Nether… But Mary and Carry agreed. They put on their best armor, grabbed their best weapons, and told Joe to open the Portal. I said I didn't want to go inside with them… But they insisted. They said the adventure would feel pointless without me. They provided me with Diamond Armor, enchanted weapons and even some good potions. Then I couldn't say no… I joined them in their quest."

"I see and you went into the Nether with them." I said.

"That's right. I joined them. But… things went off the rails really fast."

"What do you mean?"

"Joe's idea was to go in there and farm Blaze Rods. We managed to find a Nether Fortress, which was not far from the Nether Portal. However, a group of Blazes surrounded us and we had to flee the area. Carry didn't make it – he was entrapped by the Blazes and had to hide inside the Fortress. Mary came along with us, but she fell into a pit. Joe and I tried to rescue her, and that's when a Ghast attacked us out of nowhere. Joe and I ran as fast as we could. As we were approaching the

Nether Portal, Joe slipped and fell down. I tried to save him but he told me to keep running, when a bunch of Zombie Pigmen came from the lava. I was scared and I didn't know if the Zombie Pigmen would attack me, so I jumped into the Nether Portal shortly after it was shot down by a Ghast."

"Wow. Now that's bad luck right there." I said. "What happened once you were back here?"

"I… I tried going back to the Nether. However, as soon as I stepped into the Nether Portal, I was teleported to a different place inside

the Nether." She said.

"Right. Because the Nether Portal inside the Nether was damaged by a Ghast. So the Nether Portal here in the Overworld took you to a different place." I said.

"Exactly. That's why I have been crying lately. I can't make anything right… I can't even help my own friends. Then, I became Herobrine and I was tasked with two missions. Jeb told me that my friends were safe, but I had to prove myself before trying to rescue them. I failed both missions… Which means I am not ready to save my friends."

"That's why I am here, Lara." I said. "I have come here to assist you in your mission. I know being Herobrine isn't easy, but trust me – anything can be done when you put your mind to it." I comforted her.

"I really hope so, Mark." She said. "I really do…"

Day 16

It was time to get to work with Lara. She needed a lot of help not only to complete her quest, but also to overcome her biggest fear: her own lack of confidence.

"Alright Lara. Jeb said your friends are safe, correct?"

"Yes... Whatever 'safe' means inside the Nether." She said.

"Good. Rule number one: you can always trust Jeb's word. Now, we need to work on your confidence."

"I am terrible at that." She said.

"Yes, I am well aware. However, there is something you need to learn about the world, Lara. You see all those confident people out there, who just say 'I want that' and then they go for it? They just go and grab it, as if they own it?"

"Yes... Joe is like that." She said.

"Let me tell you a secret, Lara. Those people have no idea of what they're doing."

"What do you mean?" She was intrigued.

"What I mean is – they have no idea what to do. They just know that they want something. So this is rule number two in the Herobrine business, Lara. Put your mind to it! You'll never achieve anything unless you try!"

"Right..." She said.

"Honestly, I am just coming up with these rules." I said. "You know why? Because not all Herobrine rules apply to everyone else. Each person must find their own needs, their own goals, their own advantages and disadvantages over others. You have to figure out what makes you strong, what makes you stand out against others."

"Well… I am good at making pixel art." Lara said.

"That's great! I am sure we can use your skill to help in your mission." I said.

"But how?" She asked.

"Just take all of the colored wool along with us. We have a trip to the Nether to make!" I said.

Day 17

Lara took me to the Nether Portal. It was inside Joe's house.

"So this is the only Nether entrance in the area?" I asked her.

"Yes."

"Good, let's go in." I said.

We stepped into the Portal and teleported to the Nether.

"Here we are." I said. "Remember, you're the Herobrine and hostile creatures won't attack you. This means you're invulnerable

against any and all enemies in here."

"Really? I never tried that…" She said.

"Well, go on ahead! You can walk anywhere and the creatures won't bother you." I said.

She walked around and the creatures didn't bother with her. The Ghast flying nearby didn't mind us at all.

"Nice… I feel safer now." She said.

"You should. You're the Herobrine, after all!" I said. "Come on, we have a group of humans to save!"

"Where should we head to?" She asked me.

"Honestly, I don't know." I said. "Another rule of the Herobrine book: if you don't know where to go, improvise! Let's go this way first. If we don't find anything, we'll come back here and take another direction." I said.

"Well… That sounds dangerous." She said.

"We're invisible in here, Lara!" I said. "The least of our concern is our safety. We should be worried about locating your friends – we don't know if they could be in danger."

"Right… Let's get going, then." She asked me.

Day 18

We were still searching for Lara's friends, who were lost inside the Nether.

"Could you describe the area where they stayed?" I asked her.

"Uh… There was like, two lava streams flowing down next to the Portal. There was a Nether Fortress to the North of where we first arrived… and maybe a Netherrack mountain to the West? I can't be any more specific… This

place looks all the same to me."

"I agree with you, this place does look all the same." I said. "However, there must be an easier way to locate them... Well, finding a Nether Fortress is probably our best bet, right?"

"I think so." She said.

"Good! Keep an eye out for the Fortress. If we find it, we'll be much closer to finding your friends."

Lara and I walked for a few hours. Since we couldn't find anything, we decided to explore other areas of the Nether, always circling the main Nether Portal where we came from. It seemed that the new Portal had generated much farther away from the original one.

"I wish finding my friends was easier..." Lara said.

"Wait... Be careful! When you make a wish, I will have to grant it and then your friends will not be able to make any other wishes."

"Really? I can make a wish?" She asked me.

"Sure. However please remember you only have one wish, and you may need to use it only when you're in dire need." I said.

"Okay. I think I will use my wish to locate them…" Lara said.

"Sure, it's up to you." I said.

"I wish to find my friends." She said.

I snapped my fingers and a beam of light emerged in the Nether sky. We could clearly see where it was in the distance.

"I suppose that's where the Nether Fortress is!" I said.

"Nice, let's go find them." She said.

Day 19

With the huge beam of light in the skies, finding the Nether Fortress was not a hard task anymore.

"We are almost there, Lara." I said.

"Finally. I don't even know what to say to them…" She said.

"Just be honest, Lara. Tell them you were scared. Apologize for what happened." I said.

"Okay…" She replied.

We got closer to the beam of

light, and the Nether Fortress was right in front of us. Next to it, there was a

Netherrrack house which was clearly built by human hands because it stood apart from everything else inside the Nether.

"Could it be…" Lara asked.

"Definitely, Lara." I replied. "That's most likely a house built by your friends. It looks huge! That's why Jeb told you they were safe – they have been living in this house here in the Nether."

I knocked on the door while Lara stayed right behind me.

"C'mon Lara, you are the one who needs to stay in charge during this mission. Otherwise you won't pass!" I said, stepping back. "Remember, they won't recognize you in your Herobrine version. You must help them get out of here before revealing who you are."

"I understand." She said.

"Who is it?" We could hear a voice coming from the house.

"It's… it's a friend. I am here to help you." Lara said.

"Oh, just a moment." The voice was now coming over to open the door. Once it was opened, he stared at both of us for seconds before saying anything.

"Oh my. What are you two?" He asked us.

"Hello, Jo I mean, human." Lara said. "I am the Herobrine and I have come here to help you get out of the Nether."

"Herobrine? Out here at the Nether?" Joe seemed confused. "That's so weird. Of all the people I pictured rescuing us, Herobrine is the last possible one!"

"I understand this is strange,

and we apologize for coming out all of sudden. However, we have been looking for your group for quite a while. We heard you needed some help getting out of this wretched place." I intervened.

"Sure, well… I can't refuse any help. Please, come in." Joe invited us into the house. "Mary, we have visitors!" He said out loud.

"Oh, really? Who is it Oh my gosh!" Mary was surprised to see us.

"Sorry for the sudden visit." I said. "My name is Mark and I am Herobrine's assistant. This is as you can see the Herobrine herself."

"Herobrine is a girl?" Joe asked.

"Well, Herobrine can assume different genders in different servers." I said.

"Interesting." Joe said.

"Welcome to our humble abode." Mary said. "We built this house in order to stay away from the hostile mobs outside. Luckily, the Nether creatures can't destroy any blocks, apart from the Ghasts but they don't attack unless they see you."

"Very smart of you two." I said. "Where's the third human friend of yours?" I asked about Carry.

Joe and Mary looked at each other with a deep, sad expression.

"We haven't been able to retrieve Carry yet. He's still lost inside the Fortress." Joe said. "We have tried in eight different trips, but we failed to find him. We always had to return to our house before being swarmed by Blazes and other monsters."

"We believe Carry ran into the Fortress' core, deep down in the Nether, where Blazes don't spawn." Mary said. "It could take us days to get in there. It's impossible, with our current tools. We can't return to the Overworl since the Portal was destroyed."

Mary sighed.

"We are here to rescue him, too." Lara said. "We won't leave anyone behind."

"Oh, good! Thank you." Joe said. "As I said, we'll accept any help we can get."

"Could you tell us more about the Fortress itself?" I asked them.

"Sure, please sit down and we'll explain everything." Joe said.

Day 20

Joe spent the day explaining to us everything about the Nether Fortress, the main entrance, the extra rooms, the Blaze spawner locations, valuable chests and whatnot. It seemed that, despite not exploring the whole place, Mary and Joe had done a fair bit of exploration inside.

"That's all about it." Joe said.

"Interesting. Thanks for all the information." I said.

"Can you really get in there and rescue Carry?" Mary asked us.

"Yes, we can. We are invulnerable against the hostile mobs in the Nether." Lara said.

"Wow! Now talk about a huge advantage against these hostile mobs." Joe said. "We haven't had any luck because of them. Every time we go inside, a bunch of Blazes come out of nowhere and attack us."

"Don't worry, sir. We'll go there and destroy all Blaze spawners." Lara said.

"Exactly. Then new Blazes won't spawn anymore." I said.

"Thank you. That would help a lot." Joe said.

"Once we have done it, we'll proceed further into the Fortress. We will also need your help, because we don't know whether Carry will be scared to meet the Herobrine himself." I said.

"You're right… Poor Carry must be scared like a little rabbit entrapped by wolves." Joe said. "The original spawn in this world is very, very far away from where we live. No one wants to despawn and go back there. If Carry is attacked and defeated by the monsters, it will take him weeks — no, months, to walk back to our houses in the Overworld."

"Yikes, that's not a good option." I said. "Pardon my ignorance, but how can you be so sure he's still there? Hasn't he despawned yet?"

"Carry is a strong lad." Joe said. "I am sure he would never let himself be outsmarted by a bunch of angry Blazes. We'll find him alright."

"Good! We can carry on with our mission, then." I said.

Day 21

Now, it was time to put into practice all the knowledge we had obtained about the Nether Fortress.

"We'll go ahead and you two stay right behind us." I said.

"Deal." Joe said.

"Our objective this time is to go even deeper than your previous attempts." Lara said. "Please let us know in case we are going the wrong way."

"Okay, we'll inform you!" Mary replied.

We got into the Nether Fortress from the main entrance. According to Joe's description, there was a Blaze spawner not far ahead from the entrance.

"Stay still. We'll destroy the spawner first and then we can continue." I said.

Lara and I went ahead while Joe and Mary waited for us. Upon locating the spawner (with only 4 Blazes surrounding it), we destroyed everything. As predicted, the Blazes didn't attack Lara and Lara seemed more confident in her quest.

"Are you alright, Lara?" I asked her.

"Yes, I am. It's just that… I can't get rid of this feeling…" She said. "I feel guilty all the time."

"Don't think about it too much. Please, keep it up – you are doing a superb job." I encouraged her.

"Thank you." She replied, as we destroyed the last Blaze.

"Free to go!" I shouted back to Joe and Mary. They quickly ran towards us.

Going even further into the Nether Fortress, we were now searching for any clues leading up to the lost member of the group.

"Carry can't be too far in there... He is not the type who likes to take too much risk." Joe said. "However, we never found any signs of him."

"Perhaps we'll have better luck now." I said.

As we walked further into the Fortress, the place seemed to get hotter and darker.

"Gee, this place sure is getting hot." Joe said.

"It's almost like we're getting inside the lava river." Mary said.

However, there was nothing else other than the intense lava heat.

Day 22

As we progressed further into the dark alleys of the Fortress, it was almost impossible to see anything. The corridors were getting darker and Joe had to light up some torches along the way.

"Poor Carry, I wonder if he had to go through these dark areas all by himself without any visual aid." Joe said.

"Let's hope he isn't much farther into this corridor." I said.

Suddenly, we heard a scream coming down a small alley to the right.

"That's Carry's voice!" Mary said.

"Hurry up, he's is danger!" Said Joe, sprinting ahead of us. We followed him shortly after.

"There he is!" Joe said, pointing at a frail man, cornered against a wall and begging for help while a group of Blazes approached him.

"Please help me!" Carry screamed.

"Come on, Herobrine!" I told Lara.

We ran toward Carry and swiftly defeated all Blazes surrounding Carry, freeing him from their deadly attack.

"Thank you so much. I couldn't escape them any longer!" Carry said, hugging Joe and Mary. "And you are?"

"I am Herobrine." Lara said. "This is my assistant, Mark."

"Pleasure to meet you!" I said.

"They have come to help us both." Joe said.

"Herobrine himself came here to help me?!" Carry was impressed. "Well… Thank you, Herobrine. Thank you, Mark. And of course, thank you two, Mary and Joe!"

"We have been looking for you for so long, buddy!" Joe said. "Where have you been?"

"I will tell everything later. But please, let's go back! Soon enough, this place will be crowded with Blazes again…"

"Really? But we just defeated a bunch of them!" I said.

"No… Those were just a few." Carry said. "There is a place here somewhere filled with Blaze spawners! I don't know where it is… But I couldn't escape from them!"

"Please, tell us where it is and we'll go defeat them for good." I said.

"No, it's too dangerous for only two people! You can't defeat them all!" Carry alerted us.

"Don't worry, we can definitely handle it." Lara said. "You can trust us."

"Well… Alright then. I just don't want you to get hurt." Carry said.

"We won't, don't worry." I said. "However, we want to make sure all Blazes are defeated before leaving the area. You have suffered too much already – we want to leave this place in safety."

Carry explained to us where to find the Blazes, or at least, the closest location where their sounds were coming from.

Day 23

We asked Joe, Mary and Carry to stay inside a Netherrack hut we had built inside the Fortress. No matter what happened, we asked them not to leave the area until we return for them.

"Now it's you and me." I said.

"Right. Let's go get them so we can leave this place." Lara said.

We went to check the area indicated by Carry. Despite not finding any Blaze spawners, we did find some scattered Blazes in the

area.

"Let's take them down and then we proceed. If there are Blazes in here, their spawner shouldn't be too far." I said.

"Okay, I will take the ones to the right." Said Lara, grabbing her sword and heading towards the Blazes. I dealt with my share of the enemies and we got together once again to proceed onto the next corridor.

"Did you hear that?" I asked her, after hearing a sizzling noise coming from another alley.

"Yes, sounds like Blazes." Lara said.

Not far from there, we actually found the Blaze Spawners – Nine of them! The spawners were close to each other. Maybe too close to be even naturally generated, as if someone had placed them there manually.

"Have you ever seen anything like this, Lara?"

"I haven't played the game for long, but I have never seen it like this." Lara said. "Too many of them in such a small area."

"Exactly! Let's destroy all and head back to the trio." I said.

Lara and I didn't have a hard time destroying all Blaze Spanwers. Afterwards, we only had the Blazes left to defeat. Minutes later, we had cleaned the entire room.

"We are done here. Well done, Lara!" I said.

"Thank you. This wasn't hard at all." She said.

We returned to the trio to tell them of the good news. We could now return to the Nether surface after venturing so deep into the Fortress. Finally, we would be able to take them back to the Overworld through the Nether Portal!

Day 24

We met Joe, Mary and Carry patiently waiting for us at the hut.

"We're done here! All spawners destroyed." I said.

"Wow, good job guys!" Carry said.

"Thank you so much. We're feeling safer now!" Mary said.

"Let's get out of this place. I don't want to spend another day inside this cursed Fortress!" Joe said, jumping out of the hut.

We guided the trio all the way back through the small, dark corridors of the Nether Fortress. Everything seemed to be going smoothly, until…

"Wait. What is that?" Joe first noticed the little creatures crawling around our feet. There were small Magma Cubes running around. Harmless, but annoying.

"Hehe. Poor things. Must be looking for their momma." Joe said.

"Well, at least they're harmless." Mary said.

"What noise is that?" Carry asked, looking behind.

"Run, guys! Runnnnnnn!" Carry screamed, running ahead of us.

"What happened?" I asked, turning around. What I witnessed was a horde of Magma Cubes jumping fiercely towards us. There were too many to even count – we only had time to run away from them.

"Let's get out of here!" Mary said.

"Come on, let's get going!" I said. "Wait a moment… We can stay behind and protect the trio, Lara!"

"Right, let's keep them away." She said, while the other three run.

Lara and I attacked the Magma Cubes. However, these are tricky creatures – when you defeat one, they split up into four smaller parts and continue doing so until they're completely defeated. This makes the task of fighting them harder.

"Careful, some of them are slipping away from us!" I said.

"We can't leave any of them pass through us. The trio is still far from the Nether Fortress' entrance."

Lara said.

"You're right. I got it! Please hold them off a little longer." I asked Lara, while I built a cobblestone wall to keep the Magma Cubes trapped with us inside the Fortress.

"Nice. Now they can't pass through us." Lara said.

"Let's finish this now, Lara. We can't let the trio be without us – you never know what might be hiding in these hallways!" I said.

Lara and I attacked all Magma Cubes. Despite being a time-consuming task, we managed to take all of them down.

Day 25

We took down the wall and returned to our friends. They were waiting for us not too far from where they had left us.

"You guys are amazing." Carry said. "How can you defeat many monsters without a sweat?"

"Let's just say we are invulnerable against these critters." I said.

"Awesome. Thank you once again!" Carry said.

"Let's get out of here, guys. I don't want you to be entrapped by any other monster now." I said.

We guided the trio out of the Nether Fortress. Finally, Carry was no longer trapped in there!

"I never knew I would say this, but... I am actually happy to be out of the Nether Fortress." Carry said. "Thank you all so much for taking me out of there!"

"It's our pleasure!" I said.

"Our job will be over once we have taken you all out of the Nether." Lara said. "Please, follow us and we'll take you to the new Nether Portal."

"Thanks! I can't wait to step outside again." Joe said.

Day 26

While we made the walk back to the Nether Portal, the three friends talked about their adventures in the Nether.

"Man, you won't believe what I had to do to stay safe in there." Carry said. "I actually hid inside a small crevice for days. I would only go out to search for food in the chests. Luckily, I found some Apples and Bread. Other than that, I spent most of my days hidden in that hole! I knew you would be coming for me…"

"Wow that must have been tough!" Joe said.

"We went out on many different searches, Carry. It was impossible to go through those Blaze hordes." Mary said. "Luckily, we had Herobrine here to help us!"

"Exactly." Joe said. "What about Lara?"

Lara, listening quietly to the conversation.

"I haven't seen her in such a long time." Mary said. "I hope she is doing fine."

"Yeah, I was with her shortly before we got to the Portal." Joe said. "I asked her to go without me because it was too dangerous. She was lucky to pass through the Portal before that Ghast blew it up."

"Oh, so she got away safely? That's really good!" Carry said.

"Why… Why are you all so kind to her?" Lara asked.

"Well, she is our friend." Joe said.

"But it seems she abandoned you… She left you all behind. How can you be so kind?" Lara asked.

"She didn't leave us. I asked her to flee the Nether because it was too dangerous." Joe said. "In fact, Lara never wanted to come in the first place. Back then when we were attacked, I just wanted to make sure that she made it through the Portal. She didn't deserve to stay stuck here with us."

"How come she has never returned to help you?" Lara said.

"Most likely, the new Portal opened in a different area. We can't blame her." Joe said.

Lara stopped walking. The others also stopped right behind her.

"What is it, Herobrine? Is anything wrong?" Carry asked her.

"It's that… It's that…" Lara was having a hard time revealing who she was.

"It's just that this has been a tough mission." I intervened. "We're almost there, people! I am sure you'll all be happy to leave this place once and for all."

"You're right! I sure am happy to leave this place." Joe said. "Can't wait to eat some real food again."

Day 27

We found the Nether Portal this morning.

"There it is! We're near our home at last!" Mary declared.

"I can't wait to go through that Portal!" Joe said.

"Come on in guys, time to go home!" I said.

We all jumped through the Portal and returned to the Overworld.

"Home, sweet home!" Joe said.

"At long last." Carry said.

"Thank you so much for bringing us home! We'll be forever thankful to the two of you!" Mary said.

"Now, where's Lara? We ought to go after her." Joe said.

"That won't be needed, guys." I said. "Lara is right here with us."

"Really? Is she hiding somewhere?" Carry asked.

"No. I am Lara." Lara said, revealing herself to the others.

"No way... How is that possible? Your voice doesn't even sound the same!" Joe said.

"It's because of my Herobrine form. However, I was tasked with the mission of helping you three... I can't forgive myself for leaving you behind in the first place."

"Lara, you should never blame yourself for what happened." Joe said. "Like I mentioned before, I wanted to make sure you were safe. You only entered the Nether because I insisted to, so it was my duty to make sure you left safe and sound."

"Thank you, guys. Thank you so much." She said, tears rolling down her eyes.

"I am so happy to see everything went well." I said. "The friends are reunited once again! You have completed your mission with great honors, Lara. Soon enough, we'll be taken to Jeb to report about our job."

"Will you be back, Lara?" Carry asked.

"Sure, she will." I said. "In fact, she will be back as her normal self!"

"Nice. We will be waiting for you! Don't worry; we will not take any risk in the Nether anymore." Joe said.

"Thank you, guys. I can't wait to be back!" Lara said.

"And thank you, Mark. You have done an amazing job assisting our

friend Lara during these hard times."
Joe said.

"It's been my pleasure, guys. I can't express how proud I am of Lara. She has grown so much as a person in these last few days!" I said.

Shortly after saying goodbye, we were teleported back to Jeb.

Day 28

Back at the white room, Jeb greeted Lara and me.

"Welcome, and congrats. That wasn't so hard after all, was it?" Jeb asked us.

"Hello, Jeb!" I said.

"Hi." Lara said. "It wasn't hard... But it was tense. I wasn't expecting my friends to care for me so much even after I left them behind..."

"I already knew what your friends thought about you, Lara." Jeb said. "I just wanted to show you how important it is to trust yourself more and don't waste so much time thinking about things. Sometimes, the best thing to do is to trust yourself. I wanted to give you the Herobrine form so you could have an easier time rescuing your friends from the Nether."

"For that, I am thankful." Lara said. "I will always be thankful for the both of you. Mark, I wouldn't have done it without you."

"Nice job, Lara. I am very happy to see your personal growth!" I said.

Lara disappeared and Jeb talked to me about my next mission.

"Here we are now, Mark. Only two more to go." Jeb said.

"Yep. It's like a roller coaster of emotions!" I said. "Even though I have a small briefing of every mission, I never know what I am going to find."

"Be prepared, Mark. The next mission is the hardest one of all six." Jeb warned me.

"Yes, I know. I was already expecting it." I said. "But I feel much better at this job, as Coach Herobrine. I think I can handle it!"

"Great. You'll need all the experience you need." Jeb said. "Ready?"

"Ready! Bring it on!" I said.

"Good luck and I will be waiting here for your last mission!" Jeb said, snapping his fingers.

Day 29

Back in the Overworld, I woke up in a desert. There was absolutely nothing nearby indicating the presence of other humans.

"Strange… It seems Jeb brought me into a deserted area once again. I will have to look for this Klei guy…"

I walked around, searching for any signs of other people. I decided to leave the desert and go to the woods, where it would be easier to find humans. Not many people decide to build their houses or

villages in deserts.

But before I even left my spawn point, someone called me.

"Hey!" He said.

"Huh? Who is there? Where are you?" I asked, looking around.

"Psst!" The voice was calling for me.

"I can't see you!" I said out loud.

"You're Mark, right?" The voice said.

"Yes, I am. How do you know that?"

"Some guy called Klei told me about you. Come here, I will take you to him." The voice said.

"But I can't see you! Where do I have to go?" I asked the voice.

"Behind the cactus. Come over here." He said.

I walked towards the cactus and I found a strange looking guy, all dressed up in a weird costume.

"Hey. Name's Jonas." He introduced himself.

"Hi, Jonas. So, you know Klei?" I asked him.

"Yeah. He told me about you. He couldn't stay around to receive you because he had some other matters to attend to…" Jonas said.

"Really? Oh well. Anyway, can you take me to him?" I asked Jonas.

"Sure. He's waiting for you. Let's get going." Jonas said.

Day 30

Jonas and I left the desert. He was going to take me to meet Klei, the new Herobrine of my next mission.

"So, how did you meet Klei?" I asked him.

"He just came by one day, looking for someone to help." Jonas said. "He helped me a lot back in my old village, but things didn't go as planned for him. It seems he failed his mission or something, despite helping me. So I promised to help him with his next mission, as a form of paying back for his assistance."

"I see. So you must be a friend." I said.

"Yeah, I guess you can say that." Jonas said.

"So tell me Jonas, what's the deal with these three big kingdoms?" I asked him.

"I can't really tell you just yet. I will have to let Klei fill you in with the details." Jonas said.

"Okay. Fair enough." I said.

"Please, continue walking. I will catch up with you soon. I have something to check here in my backpack." Jonas said.

"Alright." I said, walking ahead of Jonas. Suddenly, I stepped on a trap and fell into a deep pit. Down there, the pit was dark but extremely wide.

"What... What happened?" I said, getting up from my fall.

"Hah! You have fallen for my trap, you silly Coach Herobrine. Now, good luck dealing with these atrocities!"

Jonas pulled a lever and the pit lit up with automated Redstone torches. Now, I could clearly see what was hiding behind the walls in that pit – Illagers trapped behind bars!

"Now, it just takes one press of a button to release all those Illagers to attack you." Jonas said.

"What are you doing, Jonas? Why do you want to hurt me?" I asked him.

"Look at me." Jonas said from the top of the pit – he took off all his clothes and revealed his true self. He was Klei, the 5th Herobrine!

"Ahahahaha. You have fallen for my trap! I managed to fool you with this stupid costume." Klei said.

"So it was you all along…" I said. "Klei, let me out of here or you'll regret it!"

"Never! You'll make my wish come true, if you want to leave that pit unscathed." Klei said.

"What is it?" I asked him.

"I wish to be the King of all three kingdoms!" Klei said. "I am done with this silly job as Herobrine. I don't want to help people – I want to be their King! They will have to bow to me!"

"Sigh… I guess this is really going to be the hardest mission of all." I said to myself.

I am trapped down the pit with angry Illagers staring at me through their cells, waiting for Klei to release them at any moment. My 5th mission was off to a bad start.

Book 6: The Last Two Missions

Day 1

Stuck in a hole and on the brink of being attacked by a horde of Illagers that was me, in a tight spot. Klei, the 5th Herobrine whom I was supposed to help, has laid down a trap to get me. He wants me to make his wish come true – he wants to be the King of all Kingdoms of the current server!

"I can't believe I fell for this silly trap…" I said.

"Well, of course you did! I am Klei; the smartest person who has ever lived. Now, will you make my wish come true? Or should I call you Coach

Herobrine? Ha ha ha!" Klei laughed out loud.

"Sigh. Of course I won't make your wish come true. Not even in a million year. Even if I wanted to, your wish would not be fulfilled because it can't be done. It's too subjective." I said.

"Fine! Then deal with the wrath of all Illagers!" Klei said, pulling the lever and releasing all angry Illagers against me.

"Sorry for cheating, Jeb but I will need a hand here..." I said. "I know this is against the rules, but I really don't want to perish to these Illagers and respawn thousands of blocks away from this spot. It would only take me longer to conclude this job..."

"Uh? Are you nuts? Who are you talking to? Jeb is not here!" Klei said.

"Absolutely, Mark." I heard Jeb's voice coming from the sky. "You've done so well, of course you also deserve for a wish of yours to come true! Let me help you."

Suddenly, all Illagers disappeared. I was teleported right in front of Klei. As for Klei, he was tied up by a magical rope.

"What is happening? Set me free!" Klei complained.

"There you go. Good luck on your mission." Jeb said again from the sky.

"Thank you a lot, Jeb. Sorry for bothering you! Now, Mr. Klei. Let's start all over again, shall we?"

"This is unfair! You're cheating! How come Jeb helps you whenever you want, but he never helps me?!" Klei said.

"The difference between you and me is crystal clear, buddy. I have been helping people ever since I became Herobrine. I did my best to assist people in need. Right now, I am doing the same, except from a different position – I am helping Herobrines with their jobs. Compared to you... Well... You're a selfish, lazy Herobrine who can't get it right. You only think of yourself and you clearly are not ready to complete your mission. The way I see it, you're just a couple of steps away from being banned forever."

"Ha, then go ahead and ban me! I am sure you would love that." Klei said.

"Absolutely not. I don't want anyone to be banned. I have a perfect record of helping people, and you're not going to be my failure. Now, I will set you free and then we can start all over again on the right foot. What

do you think about that?"

Klei didn't answer. He seemed annoyed, but much calmer.

"Alright, I will take that as a 'yes'. Now remember – if you pull any of your schemes on me again, I will have Jeb come over here and deal with you again. Stop trying to play cool and let's work together." I said.

"Whatever." Klei replied

I removed the magical ropes and Klei was free again.

"So, to proper introductions! I haven't been introduced to you yet, only to that Jonas guy. My name is Mark and I am Coach Herobrine!"

"Hmpf. I am Klei." He replied, refusing to shake hands.

"Nice to meet you, Klei." I said. "Now, where do we begin?"

Well, you tell me! You're the

smarty-pants of all the Herobrines, aren't you?"

"Sure, but I also need your cooperation. Let's go to your base, shall we?" I said.

Day 2

After insisting a little bit more, Klei finally agreed to take me to his base in this server.

"Nice place, Klei. I see you are also a good builder." I said.

"Well, of course! The best Griefer of the world must also know how to build a few blocks." Klei said.

"Alright, so tell me what you have done so far towards your goal." I asked him about his mission.

"My goal? What goal?" Klei said, eating an apple and laying on his bed. "I haven't even touched it. In fact, I have been resting here."

"Resting? But you have an important mission to complete!" I said, worried.

"Ha ha, just kidding!" Klei said. "I have already talked to the King of all three kingdoms. And guess what? They refuse to make a treaty."

"Well, I know that much…" I said. "Your objective now is to find a way to make things work."

"That's not what I do, buddy." Klei said. "I don't make things right. I only know how to destroy and cause chaos. It's not of my nature to fix things!"

"Then it will be now." I said.

Day 3

Talking to Klei was almost as hard as completing his mission. Always avoiding the main subject, evading my questions with other questions, always trying to stay one step ahead of me... Klei was a mental challenge for me.

"So, who's the 1st **King**?" I asked him.

"First of what? Who gave him the right to be the first?" Klei asked.

"I am not implying he is the first between the three. I am just asking which one of them you visited first."

"Visited? And who said I visited them? I was more like, forced to go see them!" Klei said.

"Sigh... You're annoying me." I said.

"Just kidding! Gee, can't you take a joke or two?" Klei mocked me. "Anyway, the first guy I visited was wearing this huge, golden crown. He called himself 'Arthur' and his sword's blade was embedded into a stone."

"Now, stop teasing me Klei. You're making things up. This is obviously the story of King Arthur, whose sword Excalibur was encapsulated into a stone." I said. "Tell me the truth."

"But I am telling you the truth! Trust me now, these people are nuts. You'll see for yourself once you get there. Apparently, we are in some sort of 'RPG like' server where people pick up these historical or fictional characters, and they play along. You can't even talk to them out of character!" Klei said.

"Huh... Yes, I know what an RPG server is. If that's the case, then I suppose this mission will have a little twist on itself..." I said.

"Anyway, those guys were nuts. I got out of there as soon as I could because I couldn't handle their craze." Klei said.

"Are you sure that's the reason why you left them behind?" I asked Klei.

"Well, I also pulled a few pranks during my stay, but that doesn't matter!" Klei said.

"And the **2nd King**?" I asked him.

"Uh... The 2nd King is called Merlin and he considers himself to be a magician." Klei said.

"Alright, you're obviously making fun of me." I said.

"Of course not! Well, at least not this time. I swear!" Klei said. "This guy said he left Arthur because he believed their people deserved a better treatment and he formed his own kingdom."

"Sigh. Okay, and the **3rd King**?"

"It's actually **Queen**." Klei said. "Guinevere, Arthur's former wife!"

"Really?"

"Absolutely. You'll see for yourself!" Klei said. "These three have been fighting over the control of their region for quite some time. Trust me, making them get along once again will not be easy. Not even for a Coach Herobrine like yourself."

"I know, Klei. But I am ready for this challenge." I said.

Day 4

Now that I knew about the identities of the leaders of the three kingdoms, I wanted to go visit them myself. Klei, however, didn't like the idea.

"No, let's stay here! I bet we can come up with an amazing plan to solve all problems and reunite all old friends again without ever showing our faces!"

"What do you mean, Klei? You're only making our job harder! Of course we need to meet them." I said.

"I have already done that, sir. Trust me, you're not losing anything." Klei said, anxious.

"Come on, Klei. Where exactly are their kingdoms? And tell me, what are they fighting for?"

"I will tell you everything you want to know if you promise to stay here!" Klei said.

"What? No way!" I said. "If you don't want to cooperate, then I will go search for them. I am sure finding a huge castle won't be difficult in this server."

"Wait, wait!" Klei stopped me. "Okay, you win. Let's go, I will show you where it is. But I am not coming in there with you!"

"As you wish, Klei. If I do your job without your support, you'll not be credited by Jeb." I said.

"Follow me!" Klei said,

ignoring my warning. Apparently, he really didn't want to go visit the kingdoms again for some odd reason.

Day 5

We were now heading to the castle of the 1st King, Arthur. I had to meet the King myself to make sure Klei was not pulling another one of his pranks on me. However, it's not hard to believe his story – RPG servers are widely popular these days, and I can see people taking them seriously and never dropping out of character.

However, Klei's anxiety and apparent fear of returning to the castles was unsettling. I am not sure what he has done to them, but I ought to be prepared. I suppose I will have to make things right in his namesake before even attempting to assist in this mission.

Once we are done fixing all Klei's wrongdoings, then we can proceed with the real objective – preventing a war between three kingdoms, and figuring out a way to bring peace between the Kings and the Queen.

Day 6

Despite his resistance, I convinced Klei to take me to King Arthur for a meeting.

"I am sure you are not going to like them." Klei said. "The Kings are so crazy and out of touch with reality, that they have no idea how to properly react when people from the outside come to visit them."

"That's normal. RPG servers are always loyal to their script and their characters." I said.

"Sure, you say so, but I bet

you'll change your mind upon meeting them." Klei said.

"Regardless of what I think about them, Klei, I am here to help you complete your mission. I will not be able to do so without knowing who we are dealing with." I said.

"Fair enough. Just don't tell me I didn't warn you." Klei said.

"Be honest with me, Klei. Did you do something to them? Have you pulled any of your pranks on those kingdoms?"

"Me?! Of course not! I am such a lovable person!" Klei said, but I didn't believe him.

"Right… I heard how friendly and kind you can be when you want. But as soon as people trust you, that's when you grief their servers. That's what you have done in the past, when you were the most successful griefer in the world." I

said.

"Ah, those were the days! I was having so much fun, destroying server after server." Klei said. "Too bad Jeb caught me through my IP…"

"Why don't you put those skills to good use, Klei? Why don't you use all of your knowledge and expertise to help people?" I asked him;

"Because my expertise was not made to help people, buddy!" Klei said.

Day 7

Klei and I were on the road, heading to the 1st Kingdom so I could meet King Arthur.

"How far are we, Klei?" I asked him.

"Not too far." He said.

"I hope this is not one of your tricks. Remember, I can call Jeb anytime I want if you decide to fool me once again." I warned him; however, I knew I could not keep calling Jeb whenever I wanted.

"Sure, sure. You have my word!" Klei confirmed.

"Alright. Anything else I should know before going head first into the Kingdom? Anything at all? Don't hide anything from me, Klei."

"Ah, don't be silly! It's all good, Mark. You can go ahead and meet them, no problem!" Klei reassured me.

"Okay, I will trust you." I said. "You're coming with me to talk to them."

"What? That won't be needed!" Klei seemed nervous. "You go ahead and meet the King. I can wait for you."

"You're acting strange, Klei." I said. "Like I said, either you're coming with me or I will not help you at all. Remember, we don't have much time to complete your mission."

"Okay… I will." Klei said.

Day 8

This morning, I saw a tall cobblestone tower covered by a sparkling pink glass. It was the main tower of the first Kingdom, also known as King Britannia according to Klei.

"There it is. We arrived, at last." Klei said.

"Beautiful tower! I wonder if the whole castle is equally pretty in the inside." I said.

"Oh yeah, you can bet it is." Klei said. "Pink glasses everywhere, fancy constructions and attention to the slightest details... It's truly a work of art, both the outside and the inside.

Whoever built that castle surely must be a skilled builder."

"Wonderful! Hurry, we must go talk to the King." I said.

"Remember to always address him as King Arthur at all times. Otherwise, he will be offended." Klei said.

"Okay, I understand."

Upon arriving at the gates, we saw three guards standing right outside the front wall.

"You two, over there!" The first guard yelled. "State your reason for visiting our Kingdom and tell us if you're bringing any weapons or dangerous items!"

"Hello, we are here to talk to Your Highness, King Arthur, regarding a very important matter. We are here to assist him with his disputes with the other kingdoms. And no, we are not carrying any weapons or dangerous objects." I said.

"Wait… I know you!" The second guard said, pointing at me.

"Me? I am sorry sir, but I believe that must be a mistake. I have never been here before!" I said.

"Not you, the lad behind you!" The guard said. Klei was hiding behind me, for some reason.

"Hi guys! Long time no see, uh!" He said.

"Guards, arrest that man immediately!" The third guard ordered.

"Wait! What is happening here?!" I was confused. "We are here to help!"

"You there. You will be arrested just for coming along with this criminal!" The third guard told me.

"What?! But I don't know what he did! I swear. I have no idea what is going on!" I said.

"Tell that to our people, who suffered because of the pranks and the traps spread about by this griefer." The second guard said, handcuffing Klei.

"Klei... I specifically asked you to be honest with me." I said.

"I know... It's just that... I thought they were not going to recognize me." Klei said.

"For someone who's always so smart and playful, you sure don't know how to avoid getting caught, huh." I said.

"You're the one who insisted

in bringing me here! I wanted to stay behind. This wouldn't have happened if we had followed my plan!" Klei said.

"Enough, you two!" The guard said. "We're taking you to the King. He will decide your faith!"

Day 9

Despite Klei not warning me about his shenanigans, we were about to meet the King, which was good enough for me. I just had to talk to him and make amends with the Kingdom on behalf of Klei. Or at least I would try to...

"The King, Sir Arthur, First Member of the Round Table, will receive you soon! Stay quiet and don't address the King at any moment." The first guard said, pushing us down on two chairs.

"And if the King addresses

you, always reply with 'Yes Your Honor.' Do you understand?" The second guard said.

"Sure." I said. "And you... stay quiet, Klei. I don't want you to cause even more confusion." I whispered to him.

"Me? But I am great at dealing with situations like this!" He whispered back to me.

"Uh. I doubt it." I whispered to myself.

"Sir Arthur the First Member of the Round Table, ladies and gentlemen! Bow before your King!" A man announced. Suddenly, all guards and other people around us stayed on their knees and bowed.

"Are we... Are we supposed to do anything?" Klei asked, while the both of us were handcuffed to the chairs.

"Quiet!" I said.

"Oh, benevolent, humble King. Please, cherish our unworthy days with your presence!" The announcer said. "Here, two sinners lie before you. Guide us with your eternal wisdom and smite them with thy holy powers!"

"Enough, Jake." King Arthur said. "You are a great announcer but you should take easy on the announcements."

"Okay, sir." The announcer said.

"And what do we have here?" King Arthur asked.

"Sir, these two outsiders were caught by the front gates. One of them is the guy who came about a few weeks ago and griefed the Central Area of the Kingdom, Your Honor!" The first guard said.

"Unbelievable. You did all of that, escaped the guards and then returned here, thinking you wouldn't get caught? Now that's what I call a

brave person. Either that, or just silly."
King Arthur said.

"Your Honor, if you'd allow me…" I said.

"Quiet! Never address the King, peasant!" The second guard said.

"It's okay, guys. Let's hear him out. I haven't seen this one before." King Arthur said. "And who are you? What do you want from my Kingdom?"

"My name is Mark, Your Honor. Believe it or not, but I am a coach for all the Herobrine. I and my clumsy friend here just want to help you with your problem with the other kingdoms. I know it's too much to take in, but trust me – we are also willing to compensate you for any damages caused by him during his previous… visit." I said. "I honestly didn't know what he had done, but I apologize on his behalf. I can guarantee you I will do my best to make it up…"

"Wait a moment." King Arthur interrupted me. "Coach for all Herobrines? And you two are here to help me with Merlin and Guinevere? Right. As if an outsider, who just knocked on my door, could ever help us with such a sensitive matter."

"I am aware of the absurdity of it all, sir. Just... give me a chance. I know my friend here didn't give you a good first impression, but I will do my best to make things right. Just tell me what you need help with and we'll assist you. Preventing a war between the three kingdoms is our goal." I said.

"I still don't believe in you."

King Arthur said. "I should kick you both out of this place right now. But if you really can help me with what I need... That would take a huge load off my shoulders. Come on in, I will give you guys a chance. Don't waste it, though – I will have my guards keep a close eye on both of you during your presence here."

"Thank you, King Arthur! You won't regret it!" I said. Klei remained quiet, which contributed to our admission into the Kingdom of King Arthur.

Day 10

Back at the castle, King Arthur talked to us about the dispute between the three Kingdoms.

"Finally, some privacy." King Arthur removed his crown and placed it on the table.

"Your Honor…"

"Just call me Brad." King Arthur said.

"Brad…?" I was confused.

"Yeah, short for Bradley, my real name outside this RPG server. Honestly, being a King is tiring.

Anyway, would you like to know more about this server?"

"That would be great, Your Hon... Brad." I said.

"I created this server four years ago with my two best friends. Sadly, due to some... management issues, we split up. Now we have three kingdoms and we can't agree on anything. That's what has been driving so many people away from this RPG server. To think this place once housed over 100.000 monthly active players... Now it's just an empty shell of its former self. Not even 1.000 monthly players and it is going down. What's the point in being a king and having a kingdom this big, if we don't have people living here?"

"Sorry to hear that." I said. "What can I do to help?"

"If only it was that easy." Brad said. "The reason behind our disagreement is one item: Excalibur."

"You mean, the Sword Excalibur?" I asked.

"Yes. Back when the server was at its peak, we had some of the most renowned forgers from Minecraft. The best of the best enchanters and crafters, and they managed to craft the most powerful sword I had ever laid my eyes on. Over 15 different enchantments, some of which had never been created before were placed on that sword. Honestly, I never thought such enchantments even existed in the first place! Of course, this expensive item deserved a fitting name: Excalibur."

"Impressive." I said.

"You could control the Endermen with a swing of its blade; you could change the weather by pointing it at the sky; and you could cut through Obsidian, Gold, Iron… It was truly, a masterpiece." Brad said. "And now, it's gone."

"Gone?" I asked looking at Klei, suspiciously.

"I didn't do anything, I swear!" Klei said.

"The sword was in my possession. However, as days went by, holding it in my hands was taking its toll – sometimes, my arm would hurt just by wielding it. I think it was because of the tremendous power within its blade. Then, Merlin and Guinevere said we should take turns with the sword because it was too powerful to be wielded by a single person. Of course I agreed! I would never deny that request. The sword's sheer power was too much of a burden to be carried by a single person. But then, it disappeared from my inventory – vanished! Never to be seen again. Merlin and Guinevere turned against me, claiming I had hidden the sword from them. That's when we split up."

"That's a shame. Any idea where it could have gone?" I asked him.

"No. I have sent out hundreds of expeditions looking for that cursed sword. It destroyed my long friendship with my two best friends… I wish the sword had never been created. But we can't change the past; only prevent mistakes in the future." Brad said. "Find the sword, Coach Herobrine. Bring it back to me so I can try to restore any remaining bonds with my old friends."

"I will try to do that, Brad." I said. "Come on Klei, we have a mission to complete."

"Yeah, yeah. Let's go find a sword." Klei said.

Day 11

Before searching for the sword, we also had to have a word with Brad's friends: Merlin and Guinevere.

"Let's start with Merlin, whose Kingdom is close by." I said.

"Sure." Klei said.

"You didn't play any tricks in his Kingdom, did you?" I asked him.

"No, I didn't! Only in Arthur's Kingdom." Klei said.

"Right. Let's go, then."

At the second castle, there

were no guards protecting the front gates. We didn't have any problem entering the kingdom, but the place was empty.

"Where's everyone?" I asked.

"Eerie place..." Klei commented.

We walked around the abandoned kingdom, only to find a small group of people surrounding the main castle.

"Who's coming there?" They asked.

"Mark. I am here to meet Merlin. Is he around?"

"Who are you? Spies from Arthur's Kingdom? Or are you from Guinevere's?" The other man asked.

"None. We are here in peace. Just to talk." I said.

"Turn around and leave, outsider! Or else..."

"Sigh… This will not be easy." I said.

"Halt. Who demands to talk to me?" A voice emerged from the group.

"I am here to help, sir…" I said.

"Very well. If you want to help, then go back to Arthur and tell him to give up – I will not join him again. Not until that sword is in my hands!" Merlin said from amidst the crowd.

"I am not working for King Arthur, sir. I am working for myself – I want to help your server." I said.

"Sure. You came here to help. I guess you're just like Guinevere and Arthur, then. Those two are playing their little games, laughing behind my back. I know they worked together to hide the sword from me, and now they're pretending to be enemies just so I abandon the server. Never! Did you hear me? I will never leave this place!"

And the crowd cheered.

"My loyal guards, take them out of here!" Merlin ordered, and the men came for us.

"Not that I am doubting your diplomatic skills Mark, but it's time to get out of here!" Klei said, running away from them.

"You're right. Come on!" I said, running after him.

Klei and I outran the crowd and we quickly left the second Kingdom. Obviously, we were not welcome there; so now, it was time to talk to Queen Guinevere and (hopefully) expect a better welcome party.

Day 12

Arriving at the third kingdom, we saw a big castle in a very traditional style; smaller than King Arthur's, but not less impressive and beautiful. The only guard at the front gate received us.

"Name and reason of visit, please." The guard asked.

"Uh, Mark and Klei. We are here to talk to Guinevere." I said, waiting for the worst possible reaction from the guard.

"Please, follow me." The

guard opened the gate by pushing a button behind him. The front wooden gate slowly opened up, revealing a vivid village within the gates; red brick floors, crystal clear roofs and houses made of colored wool. Villagers walking around, peacefully living their lives as if nothing bad was happening outside those gates. The village was as beautiful as the castle itself.

"The Queen is this way. She will receive you in a matter of minutes." The guard led the way.

"Things are going way too smoothly." Klei said. "At this point we should be running for our lives!"

"Shh, don't ruin this." I said. "Be gentle and respectful, not all places will treat us the same."

At the castle, Queen Guinevere herself came to receive us.

"Welcome to my Kingdom." Guinevere said. "Mark and Klei, correct?"

"Yes, Your Highness." I said. "Thanks for receiving us."

"No problem. What can I do to help you?"

"Well... We visited King Arthur and Merlin. We are here because we want to find the sword... And we want to help you three get along once again."

"Get along with those two? Hmpf." Guinevere said. "I don't think it will happen anytime soon. King Arthur keeps saying he didn't do it... The sword disappeared. Merlin has completely snapped. He doesn't trust anyone and is crazy beyond recovery. So tell me dear Mark, how do you intend to fix things?"

"I will..." I was out of ideas.

"We will find the sword and grant it to the most honorable person of the Kingdom, madam." Klei said.

"Oh, really? And who would that be?" Guinevere asked.

"We are not sure yet, but we believe only the most noble of all members should have the privilege of holding a unique item like the Excalibur. Perhaps we could embed the sword into an enchanted cobblestone block. Only the noblest of all would be able to retrieve it from the stone." Klei said.

"Oh, like in the legends, then." Queen Guinevere said, pondering. "I like that idea."

"Yes, it's the best solution for this quarrel of yours. Perhaps, we might even be able to restore Merlin's sanity in the meantime!"

"Not sure about that but I think that's a fair solution." Guinevere said. "And from me, what do you need?"

"We only need guidance on where to find the sword, Your Highness." Klei said, taking over my position. He was now fully in control of the situation, and he was good at it!

"Very well. Unfortunately like I said, the sword disappeared and I still think Arthur is the one who got rid of it." Guinevere said. "Some of my previous expeditions found clues of the sword's possible location, but we never found any concrete evidence of its whereabouts."

"Any hint would be of great help." Klei reassured her.

"Go to the West. There was a small village where some of the villagers witnessed a flying sword many months ago. The date of this event coincides with the day the sword disappeared. No one believed the villagers, but that's the only tip we have so far." Guinevere said.

"Thank you. We'll investigate right away." Klei said.

"Okay. Honestly, I just wish for all of this to be over. I don't really care about the sword anymore... But it is our only hope." Guinevere said.

We left the castle searching for new clues about the missing sword.

Our only hope was to find the answer in the West.

Day 13

Along the way, we discussed our next plans.

"So, we only have a weak hint on where to find the sword." Klei said. "The magical sword that has been gone for over a year. The sword which caused a massive turmoil between three Kingdoms and is responsible for the fall of an entire server. Did I miss anything?"

"No. It's pretty much that." I said.

"How can we have better luck at finding a freaking sword than hundreds of other players who tried the same?" Klei asked me. "Those royalties are nuts. We're never finding that sword, not even in a million year!"

"Remember we have special powers, Klei. They don't." I said.

"Yeah, well. Wait a minute… What about that one wish?" Klei said. "I can grant people one wish, can't I? Then why can't I just ask one of the Kings to wish for the sword to reappear?"

"You clearly weren't paying attention, were you?" I asked Klei.

"What do you mean?"

"King Arthur's wish is that the sword had never been created. Impossible, because we cannot change the past. Queen Guinevere's wish is for this quarrel to be over. Impossible as well, because it's too subjective. Merlin doesn't have any wishes because he has snapped."

"Oh… So we can't rely on their wishes." Klei said.

"No. This time, we'll have to do this without relying on wishes." I said.

"Can't I ask you to grant **me** one wish?" Klei asked me. "I mean, you're also a Herobrine! So each one of us can grant others one wish!"

"Well, I have already assisted other Herobrines by granting them one wish. You are right; I can also do that when the need arises. However…"

"However?" Klei asked.

"I already used my one wish in this server – remember when I asked for Jeb's help when I met you?"

"Oh… Shoot." Klei said.

"Yep. Perhaps you should stop pranking people altogether. I bet your life would be so much easier." I said.

"I mean… I didn't have any clue… I was just having fun!" Klei said.

"Well, it's water under the bridge now. Can't do anything about it we have to search for the sword on our own." I said.

Day 14

Klei and I were heading west, searching for the small village where reports of a flying sword were made on the day the sword disappeared. Some might say the residents of the village are lying, and are making it up to cover King Arthur, who hid the sword somewhere else.

However, others say that the legends are true – the sword got lost because it didn't feel at home. Only when the noblest of warriors holds its hilt, only then the sword will feel right at home! But that's just a legend as well – stories passed on by generations.

Whatever the real truth is, the sword must be found in order to restore peace in the once single Kingdom.

Day 15

The village to the West was farther than anticipated. Despite the distance, we made it to the village today.

"There it is. It's the only village in this area." I said.

"Let's go interview the residents." Klei said.

"Wait! Remember, don't scare them." I said. "Be gentle".

"Pff. Mark, I am a meet and greet expert." Klei said.

"Yeah, I guess you're right. You're just not really good at gaining people's trust, though."

"Hey!" Klei said.

We approached the village and we saw a few villagers coming out to meet us.

"Welcome! What brings you to our humble village?" One of them asked me.

"Ah, hello! We are here to ask you a few questions. Please, tell me sir – have you seen a flying sword a few months ago?"

As soon as I finished my sentence, the villagers vanished from our sight. They ran off, hiding inside their houses.

"Well done, Mr. Gentle." Klei mocked me.

"Quit it! Any idea why they ran away from me?" I asked him.

"Just think, Mark. You asked them about the flying sword. Remember what Guinevere said – hundreds of other patrols passed by this village months ago. I guess those guards were not so kind when interviewing these poor villagers." Klei said.

"Oh… Good thinking." I said. "Hello, we are not guards! Please, we are friendly. We are not here to threaten you." I tried to befriend the frightened villagers. Slowly, one by one, they left their houses.

"So… You're not a guard, right?" One of them asked.

"No. It's just the two of us. We want to find the sword, as to end this dispute between the kingdoms." I said.

"Good, good." The villager said. "We would love to help, but we can't. All we saw was a flying sword, passing by, and that's it."

"Can you tell us in which direction it went?" I asked him.

"It went that way." The villager pointed south. "There is another village in that direction, but as far I can tell, those villagers never saw any sword in that region. Now leave, please. I apologize for the impolite request, but we don't want any other guards following you and stopping by our village again."

"Sure, we'll be on our way. Thank you." I said.

We left the village and headed south. It felt like we were getting closer to our quest.

Day 16

Klei and I were searching for the new location of the missing sword. We were going from one village to the other in the hopes of finding better clues leading to the most precise location of Excalibur.

"From one village to the other... This is leading us nowhere." Klei said.

"Perhaps. But you'll never know unless you try." I said.

"Right. Are you always that optimistic?" Klei asked me.

"Yeah, pretty much." I answered. "What's the point in being

pessimistic in life? It will only stress you out more."

"Well, yes… But it's hard to be optimistic all the time." Klei said.

"Try it. You'll be surprised how easy it actually is." I said. "Look, that must be the village we're looking for.

We found the next village, which looked similar to the previous one except for two minor details – all doors were made of Iron, and the rooftops were shorter. We saw three villagers outside, talking to each other. We approached them.

"Hello, everyone. My name is Mark and this is Klei." I said. "We're here to…"

"Wait. Herobrines?!" The villager said out loud.

"What? How did you know?" I asked him.

"Herobrines?! Herobrines?!" The other villager said.

"What's going on? What are you three talking about?" I asked them.

"Come on! Follow us!" The third villager said.

For some reason, the villagers knew who we were or were expecting for our arrival. I had no clue how, or why.

Day 17

The villagers took us to a cave outside the village.

"Please go inside the cave!" One of the villagers pointed at the cave.

"Why? Can't you explain what is going on?" I asked them.

" A friend of ours! Please, save her!" The other villager said.

"Oh, your friend is trapped inside the cave? Okay... I guess we can save her." I said. "Once we are back, please tell us more about the

other Herobrines, okay?"

Klei and I entered the cave without thinking twice. We had a villager to rescue.

"These villagers aren't very eloquent like the previous ones." Klei said.

"I know. Villagers are generated by the game, but some of them are more eloquent and independent than others. I suppose these villagers must be an earlier version of the AI. Either way, we need to save their friend! Why would another villager go explode such a dark and dangerous cave all by herself?" I wondered.

"Perhaps she isn't alone. Or maybe she went looking for rare items. You know how those villagers are always looking for tradeables." Klei said.

"Indeed…" I said. "Let me know if you see or hear anything."

But the cave was as empty as it was dark. Luckily, I had brought a torch with me; I picked it up from the inventory and the cave lit up.

"Where did she go?" I pondered.

"Look!" Klei pointed at something; there were cobblestone traces on the ground.

"Someone broke through a cobblestone wall here." Klei said. "Our lost friend is not a villager, but a real human!"

"Oh. Perhaps their friend is a real human who lives with the villagers." I said. "Let's go."

Day 18

Today, we continued searching for the human lost inside the cave, but to no avail.

"She must have gone very deep into the cave. We walked all day long and found nothing!" Klei said.

"I think we're walking in circles here…" I said. "This cave is confusing. It has so many layers and pathways…"

"Is someone there?" We heard another voice coming from the back of the cave.

"Yes! Who is it? We are here to rescue you!" I replied. "Mark and Klei.

We were sent by your villagers to save you."

"Hahaha. How sweet of them to send you." The person replied, still hidden in the dark. "But I don't need any saving, my friend."

"Oh, really? You're just a normal person inside a dark cave. You know it's dangerous to walk alone without any torches. Mobs might attack you." I said.

"Don't worry. I don't have that kind of problem." She said, walking on us. This girl was a Herobrine like Klei!

"Oh, gosh. You're a Herobrine, too!" Klei was surprised, and so was I.

"So their friend was actually another Herobrine... That's why they knew we were both Herobrines, too!" I said. "Now it all makes sense."

"Wait, you two are Herobrines as well?! That's amazing! What a small world!" The girl said.

"Yeah, I mean… We weren't expecting to find another Herobrine here, neither." I said.

"Nice to meet you two. My name is Wanessa, I have been working as a Herobrine to help my village." She said.

After introducing herself, I realized who we were talking to. Wanessa, the 6th Herobrine whom I was supposed to help as soon as I completed my mission with Klei!

"Wait a minute… Wanessa?!" I said. "I am Mark, your Coach Herobrine!"

"Oh, so you're the guy who was supposed to come help me? Wonderful! Right on time, Mark. Jeb told me about you, and how you were busy helping other Herobrines." Wanessa said.

"Wait. You two already know each other?" Klei was confused.

"Not in person. Wanessa is on the list of the Herobrines I must help." I said. "She volunteered to be a Herobrine in order to help her village, and I must assist her in dealing with the Endermen attacking the village."

"You actually **volunteered** to become Herobrine? You must be crazy, girl..." Klei said. "I can't wait to get rid of this job!"

"Hahaha. I can see how tough it is for people who didn't sign up for this part, but I am actually loving it. Too bad I haven't figured out yet what is causing the Endermen to attack my village!" She said.

"We're here to help you too, Wanessa." I said.

"Hey, remember we are also on a mission! You need to help me first before helping her!" Klei said.

"Sure, I know Klei. But if I can help you both at the same time, then why not?" I said.

Day 19

We asked Wanessa what she was doing inside that cave.

"Your villagers are worried about you!" I said. "Are you looking for something?"

"Yes... The source of our doom... The thing behind all the ruckus within the Endermen." Wanessa said. "I have been looking for ways to protect my village for over a month, but the Endermen will never stop!"

"Can you tell us more about that?" I asked her.

"Sure. When I first joined this server, I spawned next to this village. Pretty lucky, right? It's not common to spawn so close to a village! Anyway, I took advantage of this opportunity and I spent my first days here, eating from their crops and living under their roof. One day I decided to leave the place and build my own home. But at that point, I had grown attached to these villagers, and the same goes to them – they loved me! I couldn't leave. I felt right at home here. So I decided to stay and make this my permanent home in this server. Everything was going just great, and then the Endermen started attacking. At first, only one or two would pop up every night. As time went by, more and more Endermen attacked our village. Nowadays, we have them coming by the dozens every single night – that's why the doors are made of Iron, and that's also why the roofs are shorter, as to prevent Endermen from teleporting into their houses."

"Wow… That's a happy story with a dark twist." Klei said.

"Indeed. These villagers mean the world to me. I didn't know what to do. As a single human living here, dealing with so many Endermen every night is a gargantuan task." Wanessa said. "I asked the developers for help. Jeb showed up and proposed me a deal – he would let me become a Herobrine for as long as I wanted in order to help my village. I accepted."

"And here you are. The 6th Herobrine!" I said.

"Yep! Things have improved a lot ever since I became Herobrine. I mean, fighting the Endermen as a Herobrine is a piece of cake. You can beat them up without ever worrying about being attacked! Pretty awesome. However, I haven't figured out what is making the Endermen angry all the time."

"Have you found any clues?" I asked her.

"There is a source of power. Something is attracting them here. Something hidden deep within this cave – something powerful, mysterious, mythical. I don't know what it is, but I have pinpointed its location based on the source of most Endermen's spawn. For the past two weeks, I have been building a long stairway leading all the way down to the last layer, where the bedrock is. However, I haven't had much luck finding the exact spot where the Endermen spawn because... You know... There are 60 layers in this cave, and I can only look after 5 to 10 at a time. The Endermen despawn within minutes, so it's a very short

window of time to work with."

"Oh... I see." I said. "In that case, we would like to help you find this source of power."

"Really? Well, thanks for the help! All support is welcome." Wanessa said.

"And I believe finding this item will prove beneficial to all of us." I said.

Day 20

Wanessa told us more about the location of the mysterious power.

"It should be down there somewhere between layers 40 to 60... I know it's quite deep because those are the only spots where I found Endermen before." Wanessa said.

"No worries, Wanessa. You did a great job. We are also looking for something in this area." I said. "And I believe this source of power might be the item we need."

"Really? What is it?" She asked me.

"It's a sword, Excalibur." I said. "It was crafted in a kingdom not far from here, in this same server. The sword is said to be gone a long time ago, and no one truly knows where it is."

"And how can you be so sure the Excalibur is here?" Klei asked.

"Remember what King Arthur told us, Klei." I said. "He mentioned how the Excalibur could control the Endermen with a swing of its blade. Perhaps the item was stashed here and now the Endermen are angrily looking for it."

"Okay… It makes sense." Klei said. "But who hid it?"

"That's a good question." I said.

"Wait. So the source of power

is an enchanted sword?" Wanessa asked me.

"Could be. It's just a guess based on our investigations so far." I said.

"I see. Well, then we should go look for it!"

"Finding the sword would put an end to a long fight between three kingdoms." I said. "Perhaps not so easily, but it's our only hope to make amends between those three former friends. Besides, even if we don't find what we are looking for, we might be able to assist you in your mission, Wanessa."

"Okay. I hope I can be of help to your mission too!" She said. "Follow me; I will take you two to the bottom layers."

Day 21

Wanessa took us to the 40th layer.

"Here we are, my friends." She said. The source of power must be between the 30th and 60th layers, as I mentioned before. I can take layers 30 to 40; Mark can keep an eye on layers 40 to 50. And Klei goes to layers 50 to 60."

"Gee, it's way too deep." Klei said.

"Yep. Shall we go there?"

"Absolutely. Lead the way." I said.

"What am I supposed to do again?" Klei asked.

"Just watch the Endermen. If you see too many of them surrounding your area, call us." I said.

"Okay… I will go to my layers." Klei said.

I went to layer 40 to stay on watch for any pesky Enderman that could show up.

Day 22

The three of us spent all night down there in the cave, each one of us inspecting a different set of layers in order to watch the Endermen. In layers 40 to 50, I didn't see a single Enderman coming up. Wanessa said that she didn't see any Endermen, either. However, Klei is the only one who reported Enderman activity in layer 58.

"Guys... You should come down here." Klei called for us from the cobblestone stairway built by Wanessa.

"Coming!" I shouted back. Wanessa and I quickly got down to where Klei was waiting for us. In layer

58, we witnessed a pack of Endermen angrily teleporting back and forth between a set of stone walls. As if they were trying to attack whatever was hiding within those walls.

"Wow... They're mad at that wall!" Klei said.

"Finally. It must be close!" Wanessa said. "Hurry, we don't have much time. The Endermen will leave as soon as the sun comes out, even if we are inside the cave. We need to search the area!"

We destroyed the walls and checked everywhere. At last, we found a glowing blade amongst the debris.

"What is that?" Klei said, grabbing the item. It exploded upon touching, leaving a hole the size of a TNT blast on the ground. Luckily, Klei wasn't harmed by the explosion because of his extra resistance for being a Herobrine, but it was a dangerous explosion.

"Careful! Don't touch it!" I warned him.

"Ouch. That hurt." Klei said, rubbing his hand against his chest.

"Is that..." Wanessa asked. "The sword?"

"It's hard to see because of all the debris from the explosion, but... It looks like a blade. It could be." I said.

"How are we going to retrieve it?" Klei asked me.

"Let me try carefully this time..." I said.

"Hey, I was careful!" Klei said.

I gently reached the blade with my right arm. I touched it with my index finger and another explosion tore the ground to pieces. I quickly jumped backwards to avoid getting hurt in the explosion.

"See? I told you I was careful!" Klei said.

"Well, I am out of ideas now." I said.

"Let me try." Wanessa said, reaching for the blade.

"No, you'll get hurt!" I warned her as she approached the cursed item, but it was too late – Wanessa had already touched the blade with her hand. The floor trembled and a small earthquake ensued;

"What... Is going on?" Klei said.

The earthquake stopped.

There were no explosions this time around, and Wanessa was now holding the blade in her hands. She removed it from the pile of debris and it was clear as the day – the item was a sword!

"That must be..." Klei said.

"It is! Excalibur, the legendary sword!" I completed his sentence.

Wanessa wasn't hurt even when she's touching the sword.

Day 23

We still don't fully comprehend why Wanessa is the only one between the three of us who can wield the sword, but we are happy nonetheless – the legendary Excalibur has been found at last!

"This sword feels so… powerful." Wanessa said, holding it.

"Careful. I don't want that thing near me! It might explode to my face!" Klei warned her.

"Don't worry, I won't touch you." Wanessa said. "Any idea why I am the only one who can hold it?"

"Honestly, no." I said. "Nevertheless, we have a simple goal for now – we'll return to your village and then we'll spend the night with this sword in hand. Let's see how the Endermen behave this time!"

"Good idea. If this truly is the culprit behind all Endermen attacks... I will be very happy to get rid of it once and for all." Wanessa said.

"Surely it would be nice if the Endermen stopped attacking the village, or if they bowed under the sword." I said. "However, we'll need your help with our own mission, Wanessa. Being the only person who's able to carry that blade around without exploding like TNT, we'll need your assistance to bring the sword back to the three kingdoms."

"Fair enough. You helped me and I will help you!" Wanessa said.

We returned to the village as to proceed with the next part of our plan.

Day 24

We spent the night at the village. As predicted, the Endermen really showed up again, but in a different behavior – they didn't attack any houses and remained calm and quiet.

"Amazing! The Endermen are not attacking the village anymore..." Wanessa said.

"Indeed. It seems the sword is the reason behind their attacks." I said.

"But that doesn't make any sense!" Klei said.

"Why not?" I asked him.

"When the sword was lost down there in the cave, the Endermen were desperately teleporting back and forth, as in an attempt to retrieve the sword from the cave. Why aren't they trying to take the sword from Wanessa?"

"Good point. Honestly, I have no idea Klei." I said. "Perhaps now that the sword has a new 'owner' – even if it's a temporary one, the Endermen feel calmer?"

"Could be..." Klei said. "So many things we don't know about this sword..."

"Now that I know my villagers will be safe, I am ready to take this sword to his original owner!" Wanessa said.

"Sure enough, let's get going then. It's not a short trip, but now we can take a shortcut through the woods. We don't have to return from the same path, because we don't need to stop by the other village on our way." I said.

Day 25

Wanessa, Klei and I were on a trip to the 1st Kingdom. Wanessa was the new bearer of the magical sword, and the only person between the three of us who could even touch it. We didn't know why the sword was behaving like that, but perhaps King Arthur would know answers to our questions.

Our objective was now simple, and yet, hard at the same time – we needed to return Excalibur to its Kingdom of origin and also find a way to make peace between the three kingdoms. King Arthur, Merlin and Guinevere must find a way to reconcile over the enchanted sword.

I don't think it will be easy...
And I don't know if placing the sword
into a magical pedestal stone and
waiting for its true owner to retrieve it
is the best idea. What if one of the
three takes the sword and the other two
don't agree with the result? What if all
three are worthy of taking the sword?
And what if none of them is?

So many questions... I can't
predict the future, so I should stop
wondering.

Day 26

We were now just a day away from the 1st Kingdom.

Talking to Wanessa and Klei, they seemed content with the outcome of our investigation – finding the Excalibur inside that cave, retrieving it from within the debris, and releasing the poor innocent village from the vile attacks of the Endermen.

However, we still didn't know who placed the sword there. Was it really all set up by King Arthur to hide the sword? Did anyone else help him? Or maybe King Arthur was telling the truth, and the sword did fly all by itself across the server, only to hide between the blocky stones of that deep cave?

It's so crazy... The more I think about this whole event, the more questions I ask myself. I don't know if I will find an answer for all of them, though...

Day 27

The big day is finally here. We arrived at the 1st Kingdom! The guards were now happy to see us, and received us with the highest honors.

"Please make way! Mr. Mark, Mr. Klei and their guest, Ms. Wanessa, have arrived with the True Sword!" They announced all over the kingdom, while escorting us.

"Is it true? The sword is back?!" One of the residents asked, staring at the sword on Wanessa's hand.

"Yes, this is the **original** Excalibur!" Klei told the villager. "Psst,

Wanessa, show them the sword! We need to show everyone!"

"Uh, right." Wanessa raised the sword, pointing at the sky. Suddenly, it started raining.

"Ohh! The real Excalibur! The sword which can change the weather!" Another local player said, after witnessing the events.

"Yes! Go tell everyone in the Kingdom. The sword is back and her rightful owner, King Arthur, will possess it once again!" The other guard said. At this point, frenzy ensued across the Kingdom – there were people everywhere, trying to take a quick peek at the sword. More guards had to come over and escort us to King Arthur's castle because of the massive commotion caused by the sword's presence.

"Your Honor!" The first guard said, at the castle's main door. "Your sword has arrived."

"Please, bring them in!" King Arthur ordered. The guard opened the door and we entered the castle's main hall.

"Welcome back, brave warriors! When we first met, I doubted you. I didn't think you would be able to help me at all. And yet, there you are – right in front of me, proving me wrong with the sword in hand!" King Arthur said.

"Thank you, Your Honor." I said.

"It wasn't easy, but we knew we would pull it off!" Klei said.

"Please, call me Brad." King Arthur said. "After your bravery and dedication, you should be allowed to call me by my real name without any formalities. And you are?" Brad said,

staring at Wanessa.

"Oh, sorry, Your Honor." Wanessa apologized. "I am Wanessa and I brought you your beloved sword!" She grabbed the sword and raised it once again. Outside the castle, the rain stopped.

"Your Honor, please be careful." I warned him. "Klei and I tried touching the sword, and it acted violently. The only person who managed to take it was Wanessa. We are not aware why this would happen, but we should let you know."

"This sword is a moody object." King Arthur said.

"Hah, so you were right, Mark." Klei said. "Perhaps the sword has a will of its own!"

"Well, I guess." I said.

"Very good! Wanessa, please come this way. I will ask you to embed the sword into the magical stone pedestal outside, which has been carefully crafted by our best alchemists and enchanters." King Arthur said.

"Wait, won't you take the sword?" I asked him.

"No. I promised Guinevere and Merlin that I would treat them fairly. Just like I promised – whoever manages to take the sword out of the pedestal, will be crowned the new King, or Queen, of our server." King Arthur said. "Now Wanessa, please place the sword into the pedestal."

"Yes, sir!" Wanessa placed the sword into the magical pedestal, emitting a purple light.

"Guards, send a messenger to Merlin's and Guinevere's Kingdom. Invite them to come over here; the final trial is ready! The sword awaits."

King Arthur said.

Day 28

The message arrived; Merlin and Guinevere were on their way to the Kingdom! All the preparations were complete, and King Arthur was waiting for his former friends to begin the new trial.

The trial of the sword would decide the faith of the server.

"Guinevere is here!" One of the guards announced. Wanessa, Klei and I were waiting outside next to the stone pedestal along with King Arthur himself. A crowd of citizens was also watching all the events

closely.

"Merlin has arrived." Another guard announced moments later. The time had come.

"Greetings, Merlin and Guinevere! Welcome to the Kingdom that was once yours." King Arthur teased them.

"Quit it, Brad." Guinevere said. "We're here for the sword, and the sword only. Spare us of your pep talks."

"The sword! The cursed sword!" Merlin said. "I want to hold it, I want to have it! Where is it?"

"It's right there, embedded into the magical stone, Merlin." Arthur said. "Whoever takes it from its resting spot will be declared the new leader. However, please be careful because the sword has been acting violently when held unworthily"

King Arthur didn't have time to finish his phrase when Merlin rushed past us and jumped right into the sword.

"It's mine! It will be mine at last!" Merlin said, grabbing the hilt with both of his hands. A huge explosion sent him flying across the patio.

"Oh my gosh!" Arthur said. "Merlin, I warned you! The sword is…"

"Mine… Mine…" Merlin moaned, trying to get on his feet again.

"Guards, take him to the hospital. The trials must continue." Arthur said.

"Yes, sir!"

"What in the world happened here?" Guinevere asked Arthur.

"The sword is unstable. It has

been, ever since it was found." Arthur said. "The magical pedestal can only keep it under control for a few seconds, so don't go grabbing it with both of your hands at the same time and you should be fine."

"Should be fine?" Guinevere asked. "Well... In that case, you can go ahead. I will go after you."

"Sure. But I'll warn you – there will be no after. The sword will come out under my grip!" Arthur bragged and positioned himself right behind the pedestal. "Behold, good people of our Kingdom! Watch your King rise once again as the one and true leader!"

King Arthur grabbed the hilt with his right hand and tried pulling the sword out of the pedestal, but it didn't move an inch.

"Gosh... What's taking it so long... Get out!" Arthur complained.

"Give up, Arthur. It's my turn now." Guinevere said.

Guinevere's was the last one of the trio, and she held the hilt with her left hand. She tried lifting the sword, but it didn't come out.

"What? Why didn't it come out?" She asked.

"I guess you're not worthy, Guinevere." Arthur said.

"If none of us is worthy, then who is?" She asked.

"Maybe the pedestal's enchantment is too strong. I will ask the alchemists to check on it later, because there must be some mistake." King Arthur said.

"Wait a moment. Can I ask something?" Klei said.

"Sure, what is it?" Arthur said.

"Let the girl try! She's the one appointed by the sword to bring it here. Let's see how the sword behaves if she tries pulling it out of the magical pedestal." Klei said.

"Nicely done, Klei." I whispered to him.

"Hah, that's silly." Arthur said. "If she manages to take the sword, than it means she's appointed to be Queen of the Kingdom!"

"Precisely, sir." Klei said. "Didn't you tell us that you wanted to let the sword decide?"

"Oh... Well..." Arthur didn't know what to do.

"Let her try." Guinevere said. "We should stop with this quarrel once and for all – let the sword decide who's worthy of being the leader, even if it's an outsider who has never lived within these gates."

"Go on, Wanessa!" I

encouraged her.

Wanessa pulled the sword out of the pedestal in a matter of seconds. She did it effortlessly, to everyone's surprise.

"Well, there it is." Klei said. "My problems here are over. Wanessa is the new Queen!"

"She has been officially chosen by the sword. Not only as its temporary carrier, but as a permanent leader. Long live the Queen!" King Arthur said, bowing to Wanessa. Guinevere did the same, and soon, everyone bowed to their new Queen.

Day 29

Word quickly spread all over the three kingdoms – a new Queen had been appointed to lead them. Accepting the decision of the sword, Guinevere, Arthur and Merlin accepted to abide by its rules to let the new Queen rule all kingdoms as if they were one.

"Queen Wanessa. From now on, you'll be leading the future of hundreds of people." Arthur said. "I bequeath the position of leader of the 1st Kingdom in your name."

"I do the same in name of the

3rd Kingdom." Guinevere said. "We have been fighting for too long for the sword's possession. Now that the sword has found its true honor, we'll respect its decision. By the way Arthur, I believe I should apologize for the way I treated you. Everything you told us was true – the sword really abandoned our Kingdom, perhaps because it felt the ever growing mistrust between the three of us. A sword as powerful as the Excalibur cannot coexist in a place filled with hatred and suspicion."

"I accept your apologies, Guinevere." Arthur said. "You're right… I guess the sword abandoned me because of my excessive pride. I should learn to be more humble. I'll start by respecting its decision to elect a new Queen."

"New Queen! New Queen!" Merlin came back from the hospital, walking on crutches. "I bequeath the 2nd Kingdom in her name. My Queen! Please take good care of us!"

"Thank you, guys." Queen Wanessa said. "Honestly, I have no

idea how to run a Kingdom! I never dreamed of being Queen, not even in a million year…"

"You'll be just fine as a Queen." Arthur said. "The sword never makes the wrong choice."

Klei and I watched the former Kings and Queen talking to their new Queen from the distance.

"Well, I guess everything went just fine in the end." Klei said to me. "I am relieved to know I didn't have to interfere between those three all by myself."

"You're lucky to have Wanessa around, Klei." I said. "She's pretty much the reason behind the happy ending for this Kingdom!"

"Yep. Oh and by the way, uh…" Klei stuttered. "Thanks for your help, Mark. I know I am not an easy person to deal with, but… I most certainly wouldn't have gotten this far without your help."

"No problem, Klei. I must say, this mission was unlike anything else I have ever done, but it was really fun." I said.

Day 30

Queen Wanessa, the new leader of the unified Kingdom, will be leading the way for a better future of this server. Perhaps with a unified Kingdom the server might return to its former glory, when it used to have hundreds of thousands of monthly players.

Since Wanessa loves her village so much, she decided to stay living there with her villager friends. The builders from the 1st Kingdom will make her a nice, cozy castle within her village and she'll guide the server from there, giving out orders and making the best of her position.

As for Klei and I, we were teleported back to Jeb's room.

"Welcome, you two." Jeb said. "What a ride, huh?"

"Hello, Jeb." I said. "That was super unexpected, but I enjoyed every minute of it."

"Uh, hi. Can I have my humanity back?" Klei asked.

"Sure, Klei. You have completed your quest, with the help from your friends. You can go now." Jeb said.

"Okay, finally!" Klei said, walking out of the room. "Oh, and before I go... Thanks again, Mark. Really appreciated it!"

"You're welcome, Klei." I replied. "I am really proud of what you've become - a Griefer to a good,

kind person. That's a huge change!"

"Ha ha, thanks. I mean, I don't know if I really changed... All I know is that I no longer feel weird when helping others. I guess it's not **that** bad after all. Anyway, see you around?" He asked me.

"Of course." I said.

Klei disappeared in a cloud of white smoke.

"Klei's coordinates will be sent to you later, just like the previous Herobrines." Jeb said. "Well Mark, I must say I am not only impressed with your performance, but I am also amused. No wonder Notch chose you to be the Herobrine of your world."

"Thank you so much, Jeb. To me, it was an honor taking part in this project once again." I said. "But after all these quests, I guess I just want to take a good rest for now…"

"Absolutely. You deserve it!" Jeb said. "I will send you back to your own server in a moment. By the way, I will also provide you with the coordinates of Wanessa's server, so you can check on her later and see if she's doing great as the new Queen."

"Thank you! And in the future, if you need me for any other missions, feel free to call. I will be happy to help!"

"Will do, Mark." Jeb said. I saw a cloud of white smoke surrounding me, as I was about to be teleported back to my own server.

"Before I go... can I ask something? Did the sword really fly all the way from Arthur's inventory to that cave next to Wanessa's home? It's kind of a coincidence I guess, unless the sword really has a mind on its own."

"No. I did that." Jeb revealed, while the white smoke covered my whole body. "That Kingdom needed a change of pace – a new leader, even. Farewell, now!"

I teleported back to my server after Jeb's reveal. I knew that whole sword story was too good to be true!

But I can't complain – everything went just fine, the way we needed. I should definitely check on all of the new friends that I made during this long journey and see how they're dealing with their new realities.

For now, a good rest is what I deserve. Good bye, my dear diary! See you later. Much, much later.

The villagers thought they came to trade items but instead the visitor griefed their village. Ann will not allow the griefers to come back to her village and destroy it again even if it means she has to take drastic measures to protect it.